The Fiddler

A Tale of Sex, Drugs and a String Quartet

RJ DODD

Books by the same author

The Stack

As co-author under the name of Chelsy Swann

Maginty's Quest
The Sandrunners

www.avantiventures.com

Published by Avanti Ventures Ltd

ISBN 978-0-9935414-0-7

Disclaimer

All characters and events depicted in this publication are entirely fictitious and any resemblance to any real person, living or dead, is entirely co-incidental.

About the author

Richard James Dodd is a professional Director of Photography in the UK TV and Film industry.

Whilst filming is his main occupation he has always had a passion for writing and has recently taken up the challenge of turning some of his own movie scripts into novels .A cinematic sense and feel of the original screenplays are very much present in all of his work.

During the course of his career he has travelled extensively around the world and now lives in Italy with his partner Mary Lou Clarke who shares the pen name Chelsy Swann.

To Mary Lou for her endless support and to Susan, editor, grateful thanks … as ever.

Chapter 1

Venice in the late 1700s

The Captain's quarters on the galleon are spacious; a wide cabin bed is at one side and comfortable upholstered chairs are placed around the room. In front of the many paned stern windows is a large table covered with sea charts held in place with the help of crystal decanters.

The cabin is quite dark and two oil lamps swing gently on their gimbals as the vessel moves slightly against the wharf side. The light from the lamps casts a glow on a blindfolded woman hanging by her wrists from one of the solid oak beams that stretch across the cabin. Her legs are tied at the ankles. Tears trickle down from under the stained white blindfold as she feebly struggles against her bindings.

Her soft sobs are slightly drowned out by the noise of the rigging slapping in the gentle breeze and the plaintive sounds of a distant violin playing a mournful tune.

The main cabin door suddenly opens and three men enter. Two of them are dusky skinned and wearing tightly wound turbans and long cloaks; the third man is shabbily dressed in an over-sized frock coat and striped silk breeches. His silver buckled shoes are missing a buckle.

Casually they approach their captive and slowly walk around her. The woman is aware of their presence and still sobbing quietly she slumps a little in her bindings.

The taller of the turbaned men moves a little closer to her and sniffs the air.

"Is she clean?"

The man in the striped breeches gives a little snort.

"Fresh from the tub. Gave her a little scrub meself…… just to make sure she was absolutely in prime condition, of course!"

Without saying anything further, the taller man slips a long bladed dagger from the folds of his cloak and moves closer to the woman who is now visibly shivering with fright. As he nears, he pulls at a slender metal chain that hangs from her neck. At the end of it is a little silver crucifix. With one swift tug the chain breaks and he throws it into a corner.

"You won't need that where you are going."

Carefully inserting the blade in the cuff of her thick grey woollen dress, he swiftly slashes the sleeve open. The woman whimpers and sags a little more. The other sleeve is cut open the same way.

The other two men take a little step back as the blade is slipped under the high collar of her dress. With one swift downward stroke the dress slides off and falls in a pile at the woman's feet.

Now completely bare and bursting into loud sobs, she tries to hide her nakedness by twisting to one side as much as she can.

All three men take their time in looking at her as she tries to move her slim and full breasted body away from their gaze.

"What do you think then?"

"One or two minor imperfections, but she will suit the purpose."

The tall man takes a breast in one hand, squeezing and fondling it. This brings more desperate sobs from the woman.

"How old?"

"The vendor says twenty years, and a virgin."

"The price is fixed." The tall man hesitates a moment and asks, "Any connections?"

"None. Abandoned as a child."

"Good, now leave me alone. There are some things I must do."

Without a word, the two other men move across to the door and step outside into the passage way.

Closing the door behind them, the small man addresses the man with the turban.

"What is he doing?"

The man merely looks at him but makes no attempt to answer.

The sound of the violin is louder out in the passage way but it is not loud enough to cover the short scream that comes from the Captain's cabin.

A few moments later the tall man steps out, closing the door behind him. He wipes his hands on a silken cloth which he then drops on the floor .

As he walks past the two men, he says to his companion, "Pay him." Then rapidly adds, "We need more like that one; same price."

The little man almost stammers in his excitement.

"That will not be a problem, Excellency. There is an endless supply."

"Good. Now get off the vessel. We sail on the turn of the tide. I will contact you when we return."

He steps back into the cabin while the other turbaned man pulls a large leather bag from a corner and opens it.

There is a clinking of glass as the trader reaches in to examine the contents.

Chapter 2

A donkey is being led up a long, winding and dusty track towards a large building at the very top of a sun baked rise. The animal, which is making slow progress, is laden with two barrels strapped to a frame that sits like a saddle across its back . The building is surrounded by large trees which cast a cooling shade over the courtyard.

Dante Gabriele pulls impatiently at the bridle rope in an effort to speed up the small beast, but his efforts produce no response. The donkey neither speeds up nor slows down. A smile plays across Dante's face. He knows this animal well and knows that it will continue at its own pace or not at all.

Dante, at eighteen, is tall, lightly muscled and deeply tanned; his face is topped by a shock of dark curly hair and his almost handsome face is noticeable mainly for his bright blue eyes, an uncommon feature in this part of Southern Italy.

He pulls gently at the donkey's ears.

"Alright, Tessy. Take your time. Nobody wants to get out of this sun and into that shade."

He leans closer and whispers in an ear, "And nobody wants to plunge its furry old face into that water trough! So, don't hurry."

The animal grunts, almost to itself, and slightly increases its pace. Dante laughs out loud.

"You are a very perverse creature, Tessy. You would make a good woman."

The pair continue on their slow hot journey and eventually reach their destination, entering the courtyard of a large country inn and way station. The yard is cobbled and Tessy's hooves make a clattering noise as she smells the water trough and resolutely heads for it.

Their arrival is noted by a large man whose stomach is covered by a stained apron. He pulls aside a beaded curtain over a door in the corner of the yard, above which is a sign proclaiming it to be the entrance to the kitchen. He watches as Dante begins to unstrap the two barrels from the donkey's back.

Angelo Nadalini, owner and chief cook at the inn, pulls aside the curtain and quietly steps out into the courtyard. He watches for a moment or two as Dante struggles to lower the barrels to the ground. When he is certain that no more effort will be needed, he speaks.

"Dante, you should have called for me. I could have helped you."

Taking a cotton handkerchief from his pocket, Dante wipes the sweat from his brow before answering.

"Signor Nadalini, how kind of you."

There is a slight hint of sarcasm as he continues, "I didn't want to disturb you. I know you are busy man."

He waves his hand to indicate the empty stable stalls.

"Running this large busy inn, horses to groom, travellers to feed."

Signor Nadalini deliberately misses the sarcasm as he wipes a hand across his bald head and smiles at Dante.

"And taking delivery of your mother's fine olive oil, best in the region."

He waves towards the kitchen door.

"Bring them in when you have recovered."

He turns to go then stops and looks back.

"By the way…."

He hesitates and mumbles, "…your room."

Dante looks at him.

"Yes?"

"You can't have it. It's taken."

Dante slowly takes this in as he looks at the empty stables. He turns back to Angelo who has swiftly disappeared back into kitchen and sprints after him.

The kitchen is large and surprisingly busy with several cooks preparing various dishes. Angelo is now at the far end and is seemingly engrossed tasting a sauce with two white hatted assistants. Dante bounds through the door and immediately spots him. Angrily pushing his way between the cooks and Angelo, he thrusts his face close to the innkeeper's.

"There is not a horse or carriage in the yard. Why can't I have my room. It is in the price for the oil."

Angelo tries to move past him but Dante blocks his way.

"We are full. There is a large group arriving tonight. Musicians, on their way to Rome. I need every room."

Dante raises his voice indignantly.

"I always stay here. I cannot get back home tonight."

Angelo is becoming annoyed at having to deal with this irritating young man.

"You can stay in the barn. This group is very important and they pay more than you do."

He turns away but Dante tugs at his shirt sleeve.

"You mean you have raised the prices for them?"

Angelo lowers his voice when he sees the kitchen staff beginning to take notice.

"Good business, that's all. You can stay in the barn for free."

He brusquely pulls Dante's hand from his shirt and returns to tasting the sauce.

Now quietly angry, Dante begins to talk in a very loud voice to Angelo's back. The man completely ignores him.

"Thank you very much, Signor Nadalini. My companion, my donkey, and I are overwhelmed by your generosity. A nice vermin infested barn to sleep in. How gracious of you."

As he says this he begins to bow from the waist and moves backwards towards the kitchen door, much to the amusement of the kitchen staff.

Chapter 3

Dante is in the barn arranging some fresh hay for his donkey, when the noise of carriages arriving in the courtyard distracts him.

Several large, horse pulled coaches are already disgorging passengers as porters from the inn dash around helping them with their luggage. The passengers seem rather noisy and flamboyant to a simple country lad like Dante and he wanders into the yard to get a closer look.

There are about twenty men and two or three women. They stand chatting and taking in the view from the terrace at the rear of the courtyard. Some of the luggage is in rather large odd shaped cases and these are handled very carefully by the porters. As Dante nears one of the carriages, attempting to get a closer look, he is suddenly hailed by someone who is standing on the roof of a vehicle.

"You there! Catch this!"

Dante turns just in time to catch a large canvas bag being thrown down from the top of the coach. He stumbles under the weight of it and almost falls to the ground.

The man on the coach speaks to him again, but this time more sternly.

"Oaf, be more careful with this one!"

Dante squints up at the man who is handing down more luggage. He takes it and recognises it as a violin case. Dante rubs his hands over the polished leather. He quickly spots the name of the maker embossed in the leather and turns to the man who has now joined him on the ground.

"It's an Amati."

Antonio, the man, is slightly older than Dante; the same height and very handsome. He has long blonde hair which is tied back with a black velvet ribbon. He is dressed in the most stylish clothes of the day and suddenly Dante feels a little awkward in his presence. He takes the case from Dante.

"You know about violins?"

"A little. Sometimes I play."

Antonio is totally disinterested.

"Really?"

He moves towards the door of the inn.

"Bring my bag."

Dante looks at the bag and then back to this somewhat arrogant stranger.

"Take it yourself. I don't work here."

Antonio stops, turns and walks back to Dante who he proceeds to look up and down.

"You don't work here?"

"No."

"Hmm, then why do you dress as though you do?"

The man's attitude throws Dante and he is slightly flustered as he answers sharply.

"I am delivering oil……from my farm."

Antonio gives Dante another long look and mumbles, "Ah, the landed gentry. How nice."

As he walks away, he motions to a porter to pick up his bag and follow him.

An irrationally annoyed Dante watches him go and then walks angrily back into the barn.

Chapter 4

The sun has set and the courtyard is dark, apart from light spilling from three large windows that look into the dining room. The sound of music and laughter drift across on the still night air and in the barn Dante listens intently.

Reluctantly he opens his small leather rucksack and pulls out some clean clothes. The faint glow from a small oil lamp casts long shadows against the wall as he changes. Finally, feeling ready to join the noisy group in the inn, he walks across to the main door.

Dante is familiar with the layout of the building; he makes his way along a corridor at the side of the dining room and enters through a narrow door.

The sight that greets him is one he has never seen in the inn before.

Large trestle tables have been arranged in a "U" shape around the crowded room. The musicians have been joined by some locals from the area and there is a small band at the far end on a small raised rostrum whose efforts at entertainment are completely drowned by the voices of the noisy guests.

Dante hesitates before moving into the room, but it is the only place to eat and he has not really eaten since breakfast. He quietly slips onto the end of a table and carefully watches events.

Antonio, the owner of the Amati violin, is sitting at the centre of the table surrounded by a number of girls who all seem to be vying for the handsome musician's attention. Suddenly some of the group sitting at the other tables start to tap cutlery on their plates. The noise grows louder and the chant of "Tonio,Tonio," begins.

At first, Antonio pretends to ignore the chants, but as the noise gets louder he shakes his head. The noise gets even louder and with feigned reluctance, Antonio rises and bows to the crowd.

To a cheer, he moves from his chair and walks to the small podium where the band are still playing. He motions for them to stop. He turns to the now rapt audience and as he does so, someone hands him a violin case. Slowly he opens it and takes out the Amati and places it on his shoulder. The crowd are now absolutely silent as Antonio begins to play.

Dante is astonished. The violinist is superb; everyone is spellbound. The piece is very short and at the abrupt end there is a moment's silence before they begin to applaud wildly. Forgetting his animosity to the man, Dante also begins to clap and continues as Antonio makes his way back to his adoring group of girls.

After a few moments, the small band resumes playing and Angelo heads a small procession of waiters pushing laden food trolleys from the kitchen. Everyone becomes engrossed with their meal. The noise level remains high as they demolish plate after plate of good food.

Dante is also absorbed with his meal, eating very quickly with his head down as he shovels forkfuls of pasta into his mouth. He is unaware for a moment or two of the figure standing across the table from him. Looking up, a curl of tomato covered pasta slowly being sucked into his mouth, he sees Antonio staring down at him.

"Ah, the fiddling farmer who is also a resident of this hostelry!"

The noise suddenly dies down as Dante acknowledges Antonio with a brief nod and then continues eating.

"I wonder if you can fiddle as well as you can farm?"

The chatter in the room stops: here is a new diversion. There is much nudging among the travellers. Their man is about to have some fun with a simple local which is always good for a laugh.

Dante is now very embarrassed at the sudden and very unwelcome attention. With a mouth full of food he can only look down at his plate trying to swallow while shaking his head. He has no idea how to handle this. Antonio, enjoying his obvious dilemma, just smiles at him.

After a few moments, Antonio speaks to him again.

"Perhaps when you have finished your meal….."

He reaches down and slides Dante's almost empty plate away from him, much to the amusement of the crowd.

"……you could play for us."

There is a little ripple of applause from the crowd. Dante is trapped. He desperately swallows his food, red faced and angry, and speaks in a low voice to Antonio.

"I don't have an instrument."

Antonio pulls a face in mock surprise and addresses the now very attentive audience.

"A fiddler without a fiddle; what an abomination."

Everyone laughs and Antonio gestures to one of his companions.

"Giorgio, see if you can find a fiddle worthy of our illustrious guest."

Giorgio quickly moves to the band and takes a violin from one of them. The instrument is battered and scratched. He hands it to Antonio who flourishes it before holding it out to a now fuming Dante.

"Not exactly an Amati, but in the hands of a Maestro it will sound just as sweet."

Dante looks around seeking an easy exit. Everyone is now looking at him and several kitchen staff are standing in the nearest doorway, blocking it. Behind them stands the imposing figure of Signor Nadalini, arms folded across his enormous chest and wearing an expectant smile. There is no escape.

More from anger than a wish to comply, Dante snatches the violin from Antonio who nods his head slightly.

"I don't know a great deal, just some religious tunes and a little Vivaldi," he mumbles timidly.

Antonio pretends to be very impressed.

"There is no choice. It must be Vivaldi."

He turns to his audience who are now enjoying every moment.

"How appropriate. How very Italian."

Taking a very reluctant Dante by the arm, Antonio leads him out into the centre of the room where he motions for silence. He points at those still sniggering and scowls in mock disapproval.

When everyone is silent he goes back to his place at the table, sits, looks around the room and then motions to Dante to begin.

Shaking slightly, Dante places the violin under his chin and lays the very tatty bow on its strings. There is now absolute silence from the crowd although one or two of the musicians are hiding smiles behind their hands.

Briefly squeezing his eyes closed Dante launches into the allegro non-molto from Vivaldi's Concerto Number 4 in F minor.

The result is astonishing. Snide looks fade from faces, smirks are replaced by frowns and then by smiles of appreciation. Antonio is almost open mouthed as he watches the young farmer make the sweetest music with an old and out of tune violin.

This is Vivaldi at its best. The previously sniggering audience are now almost mesmerized as they listen, but the biggest change is within Dante himself who now seems to be completely transported to another more beautiful place by the music. The audience no longer exists for him; he is a man with a rare talent and he displays it. There is not a sound out of anyone as he plays the piece to its conclusion.

At the end there is an even longer moment of silence than there was for Antonio's performance. And it is Antonio who breaks the silence and leaps to his feet to embrace a sweat soaked Dante. The rest of the audience break into rapturous applause and crowd around this young man who just a few minutes ago was the object of their mirth.

Holding up his hands, Antonio waits until he has everyone's attention. Then he kneels on one knee, takes Dante's hand in his and looks up at him.

"Sir, I humbly beseech you. Please tell me your name."

A flustered Dante, suspecting this is some more of Antonio's mocking games, mumbles, "Dante."

No-one moves; Antonio is still kneeling, still looking up at him.

Dante draws himself up to his full height and slowly looks around the many faces. With a new found confidence he announces in a much stronger voice.

"Dante Gabriele."

He then pulls his hand away from Antonio who smiles at him.

"Allow me to introduce myself. Antonio Benino, third violinist in the orchestra of Mr. Mozart from Vienna."

He waves his hands to indicate the rest of the group.

"Myself and this band of ne'er-do-wells are on our way to play before the Pope in Rome."

He rises and takes the battered violin from Dante.

"Signor Gabriele." He puts his hand on Dante's shoulder. "Permit me to spend the rest of this amazing evening apologizing for my appalling rudeness. Please join my group."

Dante hesitates but Antonio presses him.

"You have royally entertained us so now allow us to entertain you."

Dante is so overwhelmed by this sudden change in attitude that he allows himself to be led back to Antonio's table where he becomes the centre of attraction.

As he sits, Antonio introduces him to the man beside him, the second violinist in the orchestra, Raimondo Campese. He is a tall angular looking man with a long nose who barely acknowledges Dante with a brief nod before returning his attention to the very pretty girl sitting beside him.

A smiling Angelo Nadalini appears with a large flagon of wine which he places in front of Dante who is relaxing with his new found fame. The evening's entertainment continues.

Chapter 5

Early morning sunshine slips through the slatted walls of the barn and slowly moves across Dante's face. Without opening his eyes he turns away slightly, groaning as he does so. Slowly opening his eyes, he immediately shades them from the bright dawn light. Straw is tangled in his hair and he is still wearing the same clothes he wore the night before.

Painfully he struggles to a sitting position and takes stock of his surroundings, soon realising he is in the barn. Holding his head in both hands, he rolls over in the straw and comes face to face with Antonio who is also beginning to rouse. The violinist opens his eyes and moans loudly as he recognises Dante; the sound wakes a third sleeper, a young girl. Dante remembers her as the one who was keeping close company with Antonio's friend, the second violinist; yet here she was with Antonio.

The girl is immediately alert and hastily begins to adjust her clothes in an attempt to cover herself. Stumbling out of the deep pile of straw, she moves away when she sees where she is. Antonio laughs and clumsily tries to pull her back for another embrace, but she nimbly escapes his clutching hands as he falls back.

She leans against a stone pillar and as she finishes buttoning her dress she begins to cry softly. Dante rises to help her as she tries vainly to pull straw from the back of her hair.

Antonio's laughter is mixed with groans of pain from his hangover. As he finally begins to take in his surroundings he beckons to Dante.

"Fiddler, you are an absolute scoundrel."

Dante turns and looks at him, completely confused by what he has said.

"Taking advantage of this beautiful young lady who I happen to know had made arrangements with my immediate superior and total dimwit, Signor Campese."

Dante shakes his head.

"No, it wasn't me. I had too much wine. I'm not used to drinking so much. I can't even remember getting back here."

Antonio feigns surprise.

"Really? You didn't escort this young lady here to your quarters? It must have been me then! Sorry about that! Didn't realise this was your room."

He looks around the large barn.

"Quite spacious; you farming folks do live rather well."

"The inn is full.......of *your* orchestra. My room was given to one of them. I don't normally sleep in a barn," says Dante indignantly.

"Of course not, fiddler. Just joking." Antonio looks at him intently now. " I do remember you playing last night though. Your virtuoso piece. You are very good."

Dante gives him a brief smile. "I want to talk to you about that."

Antonio turns his attention back to the girl who is standing at the door of the barn and he replies almost dismissively.

"Really? Of course! But would you do me a favour first, as you seem to be dressed for the day."

He looks at his undone shirt and smiles again at the girl.

"Would you be so kind as to escort the young lady back to the inn, before she is missed? Raimundo Campese does not like to be crossed in matters amorous. He gets very angry."

Dante nods and takes the girl by the elbow as he helps her to open the large barn doors. Antonio sucks on a piece of straw and smiles as he watches them go.

As Dante and the girl scurry across the deserted courtyard, they are both unaware of a face in a corner window watching them. Raimundo Campese observes Dante pushing open the kitchen door and watches as the girl quickly disappears through it. When Dante starts back to the barn, the second violinist angrily lets the curtain drop and moves away from the window.

In the short time Dante has been away, Antonio has gone back to sleep and is not too pleased when he is roughly shaken awake. He sits up in the straw and watches as Dante begins packing some of his possessions into a small leather bag.

"Do you think I could become a musician?"

Antonio notices the excitement in Dante's voice. He moans slightly and puts his head in his hands.

"Anyone can."

"I know that. But good enough to join an orchestra?"

"Most people would never become that skilled."

Dante is now attending to the donkey and he places a blanket over its back before putting on the wooden harness.

"But last night you said I was good enough to play alongside you."

"Never trust a musician, particularly when he is drunk."

Dante stops what he is doing and turns sharply to look at him.

"So you lied?"

Antonio squints at Dante through his fingers.

"No, I didn't lie. You are very capable, but you are not trained. It takes years of studying before you can even be considered for a place in an orchestra. And there are a lot of talented musicians chasing very few positions."

"I could train."

Antonio begins to pluck straw from his clothes.

"Stay with what you are good at, Dante. Farming. At least you will always be able to eat."

Dante strokes the ears of the little donkey and looks straight at Antonio.

"In my life you are born a farmer and you die a farmer. Most people accept that and are happy with it, but I have always wanted to play music, the very best music. Last night made me realise I am capable of doing that. I have never played in front of real musicians before."

He carefully considers his next sentence.

"I want to become one of you."

Antonio has heard enough of Dante's yearnings and is getting irritated.

"Let me explain something to you. I will speak very slowly and make allowance for your country ways."

Dante just raises his eyebrows at the insult as Antonio continues.

"If we get it wrong on the night then we are out. It is enormously stressful. Why do you think we half kill ourselves with drink like we did last night?"

Dante does not respond, but continues to look straight at him.

"Dante, take my advice and stay away. It is a life that is attractive only to idiots."

Again there is no response from Dante.

"You are a talented musician, but you are also a fool. You know some church music and have a knowledge of Vivaldi, but as a professional you must be able to play everyone's music. Mozart's music is massively complex. You would last two minutes."

He shakes his head in exasperation.

"We rehearse for weeks just to get one piece right and...."

Dante cuts him off.

"Will you help me?"

Antonio looks at him, throws his hands into the air and falls back into the straw.

"Well, you passed the idiot test in some style."

He takes a moment or two to gather his thoughts and then with a resigned air continues.

"Mozart is giving the first concert at the Theatre Argentina in Rome in ten days. Until then we will be in rehearsal."

He sits up and with some emphasis adds.

"You will not get a job as a musician, but there might be some work with the waggoners. I will see what I can do."

Dante's face breaks into a grin.

Antonio's voice now takes on a sarcastic tone.

"If you are determined to destroy your life, then allow me to be the one to assist you."

Dante rapidly walks across to a surprised Antonio and grabs him by the shoulder.

"Thank you, Antonio. I won't let you down. I'll be there…."

He hesitates slightly.

"….somehow."

He turns to the donkey, puts the now empty barrel holder on and leads the animal to the door.

Antonio watches him go and murmurs to himself, "Not if you have any sense."

Dante pushes the large doors wide open, sits side saddle on the small animal and whips it gently until it finally bursts into a little trot and moves across the courtyard to the dusty track leading down the hill.

He has travelled a few hundred yards and is about to disappear round a bend and out of sight, when an irate second violinist in the form of Raimundo Campese bursts through the inn doors and into the courtyard.

Still pulling his shirt on with one hand and dragging the weeping girl from the barn with the other, he watches the donkey and its passenger disappear round the bend. Realising he has no chance of catching up with them, he screams abuse and curses in his rage.

Antonio, on hearing the noise, moves swiftly to an open barn window and watches the scene.

"Stay on the farm, young fiddler. This is no world for you," he chuckles.

Still watching he takes a small green glass bottle from his pocket, uncorks it and takes a sip.

Chapter 6

Dante crashes with a sickening thud against the stone kitchen wall. As he reels forward, stunned by the impact, strong hands grab him by the shirt front and throw him back. Franco Gabriele is a broad shouldered muscular man and his son is not able to resist him physically. But Dante's mother, Anna, is. She forces herself between the two men as she shouts to one of her three younger children in the room.

"Bruno, fetch Emanuele! Quickly!"

Bruno, the eldest of the three small children, dashes from the room whilst the other two seek refuge behind what small pieces of furniture there are in the sparsely equipped farm kitchen. From here they continue to witness this terrible and frightening family dispute.

Anna pushes her husband far enough away from his son so that his wildly swinging fists can't reach him; Dante staggers to the far end of the kitchen table where he collapses into a chair. His father continues to attack him with angry words.

Out in the farmyard, Dante's donkey is still tied to a ring in the wall and it moves out of the way as, a few minutes later, Bruno comes dashing back from his errand, followed by a priest who is moving so fast that his long black robes billow out behind him. Bruno stops at the door and waits until the priest sweeps past him and into the house.

Dante is still sitting at the end of the long table and his mother dabs at a small cut above his eye with a damp cloth. His father stands in front of the large stone fireplace at the other end of the room, his arms folded tightly across his chest. The violence has ceased, but there is still a strained atmosphere in the room as Father Emanuele Gabriele enters.

Dante stares at the table and his father avoids eye contact with the priest. Anna breaks the silence.

"These two fools have been fighting."

The priest nods.

"I can see that," he says quietly.

There is a moment or two more of silence then he speaks again.

"Do I have to guess why?"

All three of them begin to speak at once, but the priest holds up his hand for silence and then nods to Anna to continue. She places her hand on Dante's head as she speaks.

"He wants to leave home."

Her remark brings forth another tirade of invective from Franco, but a glance from Emanuele silences him.

"Why?"

Franco cannot contain his anger.

"Because he is a stupid selfish fool."

Emanuele turns to him and says firmly, "Franco, please."

He motions for Anna to speak.

"He wants to become a musician."

Franco suddenly points at the priest.

"I blame you for this. You and that damned violin."

A shocked Anna shouts at him.

"Franco, do not curse in front of the Father and do not swear in my house."

Still fuming, Franco turns to her.

"On Sundays and at the church he is the priest and a Father; here in my home, he is my brother."

The priest speaks quietly.

"Your elder brother, and in both capacities I am here to help."

Franco once again averts his eyes. Emanuele walks over to him and puts an arm around his shoulder.

"Franco. Why don't we go outside? We need to talk."

Franco sullenly considers this request for a moment and then with a dark look at his son and wife, he brusquely leaves the room. The priest also looks at Anna, shrugs his shoulders, smiles and then follows his younger brother out into the sunlit yard.

Chapter 7

A short while later, on a small hillock overlooking the farm and nearby village, the brothers - priest and farmer - sit in silence as they contemplate the view. The two of them are sitting close together and it is Franco who eventually breaks the silence.

"He didn't even take the harness off the donkey."

There is no reaction from the priest and Franco continues.

"He came dashing in, all excited. Thought we would be pleased. Pleased that he wanted to leave us, leave all of this."

He almost chokes on the next sentence.

"To play music."

Emanuele nods as his brother lets his anger and frustration come out.

"He is a farmer's son."

He waves his hand to indicate the farm below them on the hillside. "This will be his one day. His inheritance, like it was mine."

Emanuele turns to him and says softly, "Like it was my inheritance, you mean?"

For the first time Franco half smiles.

"True."

"Ironic really. You got the 'damned violin' and I got the farm!"

The two brothers share a memory which brings a slight smile to both of them.

Emanuele picks up a small pebble and idly throws it down into the valley.

"You were always the farmer and I was the violinist. Why couldn't Papa see that?"

"It is never questioned by anyone. The land always goes to the first born."

Emanuele gives a little laugh.

"Remember the rows? He threatened to give the entire place to the poor nuns' convent. Throw us both out."

Franco smiles at the memory as Emanuele carries on reminiscing.

"For years I had been telling him I wanted to be a priest. I would stay at home studying and playing the violin, while you went out into the fields with him to make this place what it is."

"I went out into the fields to get away from that screeching violin. You were terrible!"

Both men laugh out loud at the memory.

"Emanuele, Papa would turn in his grave if he knew what we did."

"My calling convinces me that he does know."

"Does he approve?"

"Of course he does. It makes absolute sense."

Emanuele points to the farm below them.

"You wanted to farm and raise a family. I wanted to become a priest, and improve my musical skills. The pity is that we had to wait until he died before we could both do what we wanted to do."

Franco nods.

"We were very discreet, very subtle."

Emanuele agrees.

"There comes a time when you can become too subtle. We almost waited too long. I remember being the oldest novitiate in the seminary. There were Cardinals younger than me. The church almost refused to award me a parish. 'Too old', they said!"

"Anna and I started a family."

"You needed a home. I think you got a bargain. A farm for a violin."

Franco slowly reaches over and puts his hand on top of his brother's hand. The contrast is marked. The farmer's large calloused, scarred and suntanned hand is almost as big as both of his brother's.

"And a wonderful priest for a brother."

Both of them settle into their own thoughts and then Emanuele speaks.

"Will you let him go?"

Franco considers his answer for a moment.

"Sadly, I can't really stop him. When I tried to talk some sense into him, he said there was nothing I could say or do that would keep him here. It was his life and he would lead it as he saw fit. It's the first time he has ever talked back to me. That's when I got angry and started to hit him."

"It is sad that it has come to this."

Franco grins.

"The shock was when he started to hit me back."

Another short silence and then Emanuele puts one of his hands on top of his brother's and turns to him.

"It's an age old problem. Too many cockerels in the coop! Franco, Bruno is the farmer. He will do a better job of it than Dante. Give the boy your blessing and let him go. He may surprise you and return one day, rich and famous."

Franco nods in agreement and says quietly, "My fear though is that he may never return."

Emanuele puts an arm around his brother's shoulder to comfort him and in silence they both stare out over the valley.

Chapter 8

The parish church which sits at the top of a small slope in the square is not large, yet it almost dwarfs the modest houses set around it. Inside the pews are arranged in lines, one row either side of the central aisle. Dante is sitting close to the front in a ray of sunlight that manages to filter through the grime covered window set high in the wall.

The silence of the church is broken when Emanuele pushes open the large door and moves down the church to sit beside his nephew. He is the first to speak.

"How is your face?"

Dante grimaces as he tenderly touches his chin.

"Sore."

The priest smiles.

"Your father always had a hard fist. I never had any trouble from the local bully boys."

Dante turns to look at him.

"Why should they bother you?"

"A farm boy who played a violin. Against the natural order of things."

He pauses and adds, "Funny thing is, I have married most of them off, baptized their children and held their funerals, all in this little church. They don't seem to mind me now."

Carefully touching his bruised lip, Dante winces slightly.

"They probably remember his hard fists. What did Dad say?"

"He is sad; he loves you and thinks he will lose you. He really wanted you to take over the farm when the time comes."

Dante moves to say something, but Emanuele stops him.

"I told him you were not a farmer. Bruno is."

He takes one of Dante's hands in his.

"These are a violinist's hands. Two more years working the land and they will become useless for anything else."

"I tried to tell him that."

Emanuele gives a little laugh.

"I said that one day you might become rich and famous."

Dante stands and faces his uncle.

"This isn't about fame or money; it's about something else. Achievement maybe, or finding out who I am and what I can do from my efforts."

Emanuele looks intently into the face of his young nephew.

"You sound like someone I know very well."

"What happened to him?"

"I think in the end he got what he wanted, but he almost left it too late."

"It doesn't matter as long as he is happy."

Emanuele takes a moment or two before he nods in agreement, then asks, "When do you leave?"

"I have to be in Rome in two days, so I thought I would go early tomorrow morning."

"So soon? How sad."

Uncle and nephew sit in silence for a few moments, contemplating what this means and then Emanuele rises.

"Will you play for me one last time before you go?"

"Of course."

Emanuele, anticipating this answer is already on his way to a small door set at the side of the altar. Within a few moments he returns, carrying a battered old violin case. He hands it to Dante as he sits down again.

"My favourite piece, Maestro."

Dante lovingly removes the old violin from its case and rubs it gently with the soft cloth that covers it. He walks to the front of the altar and begins to play the Largo from Vivaldi's L'Inverno.

The music fills the empty church and the slight echo seems to add a surreal quality. His uncle leans back in the pew, closes his eyes and lets the sweet sound wash over him.

Unknown to either one of them, Franco is sitting on the stone steps outside the large door. Like his brother, he leans his head against the old timbers and listens, a tear slowly rolls down his cheek.

Dante soon finishes the short piece and waits for the echo to fade away before he takes the violin from under his chin. Emanuele, gently applauding, gets to his feet and gives his nephew a hug. Then he takes the violin from him, places it in the old battered case and with a slight flourish hands it back to a mystified Dante.

"Take it, Dante. It is yours."

A stunned Dante shakes his head.

"Impossible."

Emanuele speaks to him gently but firmly.

"It belongs with its rightful owner. I cannot make it sound like you can and you cannot be a fiddler without a fiddle. I also promised your father that I would take your place in the fields when he needs me."

He looks at his outspread hands.

"Won't take much of that before I won't be able to play it at all."

A shaken Dante pushes the case back to his uncle.

"But it's all you own."

Emanuele smiles at him.

"Priests take a vow of poverty, no personal possessions. I really shouldn't have it at all and if you take it then it still belongs to the family."

Dante lowers his voice and quickly glances around him.

"But it's a De Munk. Probably worth more than the farm."

Mimicking his nephew's actions and with a look of mock horror on his face, Emanuele also quickly scans the deserted interior of the church.

"We must not let your father know that," he whispers. "He thinks it's just an old fiddle."

He pauses for a moment.

"And I always felt you would follow in my musical footsteps, even perhaps into the priesthood."

Dante smiles at the suggestion.

"Me? A priest? I would never consider myself devout enough."

He looks at the violin case, then hands it back.

"I would also like to raise a family one day."

Emanuele firmly pushes the case back to Dante who reluctantly takes it and hugs it to his chest.

"Thank you, uncle. I will guard it with my life."

The two men savour the moment, then Emanuele says, as he reaches into the side of his dark robe, "I do have a little money."

He holds up his hand to stop the protest already forming within his nephew.

"It is not a lot and I must remember my vow of poverty."

He hands over a small leather purse.

"Think of it as a loan and you can make a donation to the church when you begin to earn some money of your own."

They embrace for the last time and as Dante begins to walk towards the door, Emanuele calls out, "Try to forgive your father, Dante. He means well. I will keep in touch. Take care." Then almost to himself he adds, "Satisfy your soul, Dante."

Dante is too emotionally charged to be able to speak and can only turn and wave farewell when he reaches the open door.

Chapter 9

The early morning is cold, not yet warm enough to burn off the slight mist that surrounds the Gabriele farm.

Chickens scatter away as the front door opens and Anna steps out, closely followed by her two youngest children. The little girl is crying and the smallest child clings to his mother's skirt as Dante steps out of the old farmhouse.

No-one is saying much and Dante bends down to kiss his little brother and sister. Anna simply gives him a hug when he stands up. She holds him tight, reluctant to let him go, then suddenly releases him. It is an awkward moment for son and mother and Dante struggles to hold back a tear.

"Where are father and Bruno?"

Dabbing her face with a handkerchief, Anna can barely speak.

"In the fields. Your father said he has some urgent work to do. They left before daybreak. You might see them on the way out. Bruno said to enjoy the adventure and not to get back too soon."

She smiles.

"He is taking your room. Getting away from these two."

She pats the youngsters on their heads.

"And your father gives you his love and blessing. He said to tell you that his mind wants to tell you never to come back, but his heart says this will always be your home."

As he hears these words Dante is incapable of speech and just nods. With a quick hug and a kiss on his mother's cheek he abruptly turns and strides out of the farm yard quickly making his way up the small incline to the main road and out of sight of the farm.

As he reaches the top of the hill he turns to wave but his mother and the children are nowhere to be seen and the chickens have gone back to pecking for food around the now closed kitchen door.

After walking for a few hundred yards, he sees his father and Bruno working in the olive grove. Bruno spots him and begins to wave; Dante waves back and watches as Bruno draws his father's attention.

Franco turns and looks at Dante. He carefully unties a small neckerchief from around his neck and is about to wave with it when he hesitates and then wipes the sweat from his brow. The two men hold this long distance look for a few moments then Franco urges Bruno to get back to work and turns his back on his eldest son.

Dante, who has been waving his old battered hat, sadly lowers it. He continues to watch for a few seconds longer and then for the last time he turns and determinedly sets out on his journey to Rome.

Chapter 10

It is early evening and the first stage of Dante's journey is almost over. Once again he trudges up the long slope to Signor Nadalini's inn.

Unusually there are several small groups of people walking up the track, an air of excitement and urgency among them. Several carriages move swiftly past him; the sound of laughter and music drifts down towards him and he quickens his pace.

When he arrives at the inn, the courtyard is already crammed with horses and ornately decorated carriages, very different from the shabby ones that had transported Antonio and his orchestral companions. These are the carriages of the wealthy. Their liveried drivers are congregated at a long trestle table where food is being laid out for them; the way they are devouring every dish suggests they have obviously travelled a long way.

Skirting around this small group of hungry men, Dante slips through a door in the corner of the yard that leads directly into the kitchen area. He almost immediately bumps into Signor Nadalini. The man is not pleased to see him. He is sporting a very swollen black eye.

"What do you want?" he growls, grabbing Dante roughly by the shirt.

"A room."

Dante looks closely at Signor Nadalini.

"What happened to your eye?"

Signor Nadalini pushes his face close to Dante.

"You should know. You are the cause of it. And for you there is definitely no room at the inn."

He shoves the young man away. Dante is completely puzzled by his treatment.

"Why, Angelo? Why?"

Angelo Nadalini struggles to keep his temper.

"You. You and those thug musicians. After you scuttled off home, the one who calls himself Raimundo Campese, accused me of encouraging you to steal his girlfriend. Said I plied him with cheap wine in order to help you."

He carefully touches his bruised face.

"For a violinist he has a very nasty temper."

Dante tries to hide a little smile.

"It had nothing to do with me. She was with Antonio."

This remark does not please the innkeeper and in a slight fit of rage he continues.

"He's another one. Tried to cheat me out of paying for some wine he had ordered; said I had miscounted the bottles."

His face goes an even deeper shade of red.

"Said it was rubbish wine and I had overcharged. Me….."

Angelo Nadalini is now in full flight and he carries on.

"……As far as I am concerned, musicians are the scum of the earth. No manners, no breeding, thieves and cutthroats to a man."

He calms down slightly now he has unloaded his bile.

"Not like the party we have staying tonight."

Dante is slightly disappointed to have it confirmed that Antonio had moved on. He had hoped to beg a lift.

"Who are they?"

Angelo preens slightly.

"Aristocracy."

Dante pulls a suitably impressed face as Angelo continues.

"At least they know how to behave."

As he finishes saying this, there is a large cheer from the dining room and a young waitress dashes out into the corridor, wiping a tear from her eyes. She storms past the two men pulling her apron off as she goes and without stopping she throws the garment onto the floor and runs out into the courtyard.

An elderly looking waitress pokes her head into the corridor from the dining room and sees Angelo.

"He got her a good one there. Skirt went straight over her head."

She laughs.

"Poor girl. Had no idea what to do. Started crying."

Angelo puts his head in hands and groans.

"Nooo! That's the third one that's gone tonight. Anymore and I will have to finish up serving myself."

A bemused Dante asks, "What's happening?"

Angelo leans against the wall slightly deflated.

"We have the Countess Margarethe Waldstadten from Vienna staying. The most gracious of women."

He pauses, looks both ways, lowers his voice, and adds, "Unfortunately, her entertainer is amusing only to her and himself."

He turns to the older waitress.

"Where is he now?"

She peers into the room.

"Can't see him; he is probably hiding from you."

Angelo gives out another groan. Dante seizes his chance.

"Give me a room and I'll serve dishes for you."

Angelo slowly turns to look at him. While trying to work out what the catch is, he suddenly spots the Violin case sticking out of the top of Dante's bag.

"Is that a fiddle?"

"It is a violin. I am joining up with Antonio and going to Rome." And with some pride he adds, "To become a professional violinist."

Angelo looks at him shaking his head.

"You must be mad! Fiddle or violin they are both the same to me, and I have a better idea."

He grabs Dante by his jacket lapel and pulls him towards the door leading to the dining hall.

The scene in the grand room is much the same as it was two evenings ago except there is a high backed chair placed at the centre of the top table. The chair is draped in red and gold silk in order to resemble a throne.

Seated on this throne is a woman who, from a distance, appears to be aged between fifty and sixty; she is surrounded by a large group of people dressed in the manner of courtiers, silken jackets and striped hose and extravagant wigs, and the men in the group are as heavily made up as the women. All of them are very drunk and vying to catch the eye of the woman on the throne.

Dante takes a long look and then starts to back out into the kitchen corridor. Angelo Nadalini tightens his grip on his jacket and leans close to his face.

"You want a room?"

Dante nods.

"Ok then. Play for the Countess and I will get you one!"

Dante shakes his head.

"It's fine. I will stay in the barn again."

"You can't. It's full."

"Then the rooms must be, too."

"You can share."

"Who with?"

Angelo relaxes his grip slightly and forces a smile on his sweaty face.

"Don't you worry; leave that to me. Hurry lad. Is it a deal?"

He looks intently into Dante's eyes and almost pleads with him.

"I have to catch that bloody entertainer before he ruins me. If he messes with one of the local gentry's wives then I might as well close the place down, that is if I live that long."

For a fleeting moment Dante almost feels a twinge of pity for the man, but soon remembers who he is dealing with and he presses his advantage.

"And food, and drink."

Angelo screws up his face as if in great pain. Then, forcing a smile, he urges, "Get that fiddle out lad! This will be your first paid engagement, and for royalty."

Still keeping a grip on Dante, Angelo pulls him gently through the crowd and forces his way through to the

Countess. Avoiding some of her followers who are performing a wild dance in the middle of the room, Angelo makes an exaggerated and deep bow in front of her as he introduces Dante.

"Countess, allow me to introduce a young protégé of mine whose services I have acquired, at enormous cost, to entertain you and your party. He is about to join your fellow countryman Signor Mozart in Rome for his series of concerts before the Pope. Signor Dante Gabriele; violinist."

Dante is busy removing his violin from the bag when he hears his name. He hurriedly stops and copies Angelo with a deep bow.

He then stands to look at the Countess at close quarters for the first time. From a distance she seemed so much younger but now close up he gets a shock as she takes his outstretched hand. The Countess is extremely old and looks it; her deeply wrinkled face is covered in thick, badly applied, patches of makeup. She looks closely at Dante for a second or two and obviously liking what she sees, she smiles at him.

Dante reels back as she displays a row of blackened wooden teeth. Her eyes almost disappear into the mass of wrinkles that seem to bunch up on her face. Still holding his hand, she turns to Angelo who is standing behind Dante, slyly holding on to the young man's breeches.

"Delightful."

She turns back to Dante.

"Dear, sweet Wolfgang. Do give him my regards and tell him that I shall be in Rome for all of his concerts with all of my dear friends."

She waves a fan to indicate the now rowdy drunks who are attempting to dance to the music from the same band of musicians from two nights ago.

"Now, which of his pieces are you going to play?"

Still shocked from being so close to this aristocratic old crone, Dante panics slightly at the question and Angelo twists his belt tighter.

Realising he is trapped, Dante forces his brain to work quickly.

"Well, Countess, in view of the fact that you will be hearing all of Signor Mozart's works in Rome, it occurs to me that something from an Italian composer might be fitting. Our own Signor Vivaldi is my suggestion."

The Countess smiles at him again and, surprisingly for an old woman, squeezes his hand very tightly.

"How thoughtful of you."

Angelo, having done his duty, releases Dante's belt and backs away. The Countess continues as she looks around the room.

"But before you begin I wish to have my dear friend and companion with me."

She turns to Dante again.

"I am sure you two will get along, as you are both entertainers. He is such a sweet dear thing, does absolutely everything for me; a great comfort."

The Countess looks around the room again for her companion and when she can't see him she bellows at the top of her voice, "Giacomo Grande! Come here, at once!"

Dante catches the full force of her voice which is accompanied by a few gobbets of saliva and a wave of halitosis. He backs away from her as she prepares to shout again. Out of the line of fire, he busies himself preparing his violin.

He is totally unprepared when at the end of her second bellow her voluminous skirts billow out and a dwarf about three feet tall jumps out and lands in front of him.

The dwarf's face is made up to look like a clown with a bright red nose and red rouge spots on his cheeks; he is wearing a three pointed floppy hat with bells sewn onto the end of each point.

He leans forward to get close to Dante and in a very loud voice says, "Giacomo Grande, entertainer to the nobility and everything else besides."

As he introduces himself, he strokes a long purple codpiece, at least a foot long, that sticks out from his crutch.

He then holds out his hand to Dante who instinctively reaches out to shake it. Their hands are almost touching when the dwarf whips his away and pushes up his codpiece. Unwittingly, Dante holds it for a moment, soon realising his mistake. This is obviously one of the Dwarf's party pieces and the drunken crowd with the Countess burst out laughing.

No sooner has he done this than he swiftly moves around behind Dante. He thrusts a hand between his legs and grabs his genitals, gives them a long hard squeeze causing Dante to fall to his knees in pain. Letting go quickly, he jumps up onto the knee of the Countess where he sits and grins inanely at a now very embarrassed Dante.

The Countess leans over and whispers to him, "Isn't he just adorable? So funny? Play when you please, Signor Dante."

Taking a few moments to recover both his breath and his composure, Dante at last prepares to play.

The sound of the Allegro from Concerto No. 1 E major 'La Primavera' begins to filter through the background noise in the room and the chatter of the rowdy crowd subsides as they become aware of his playing; they begin to pay attention to the young musician.

This is not to the liking of the usual centre of attention at these events and Giacomo Grande decides he will spice up the performance a little. The dwarf yawns widely and then strokes his codpiece. Failing to attract the attention of his mistress, he kisses her ear and pushes his tongue into it. She completely ignores him.

He slides down from her knee and disappears behind her chair. A moment later a puppet which bears a grotesque but accurate resemblance to the Countess, pops up over her shoulder. The puppet is waved from side to side, with the unkempt wig flowing out at both sides. She is oblivious to it but there are some smirks from those who do spot it. Not enough for the dwarf though and he throws it to one side.

The Countess is completely absorbed by Dante and his music and when Giacomo Grande runs behind him and shoves his codpiece between his legs, she impatiently waves him away. The dwarf is not amused by this and crossly slinks off to stand behind her chair.

When Dante finally finishes the music he is enthusiastically applauded, mainly by the Countess. All of her guests continue to applaud politely as she rises from her makeshift throne, walks over to Dante and much to his disgust embraces him and gives him a very wet and lingering kiss on his cheek. He is then led to a chair beside hers and when he is seated she places her bony hand on his thigh.

Both Giacomo Grande and Angelo see this and both react differently.

Angelo slides up behind Dante, places a large bottle of wine in front of him and whispers in his ear, "Funny people, the aristocracy. The only way to get through this is to get blind drunk like the rest of them."

Giacomo Grande reappears from behind the chair and moves out onto the dance floor. He has tied mirrors to his shoes and he follows behind some of the dancing females trying to look up their skirts.

Angelo sees him and begins to chase the little man who is very nimble and manages to keep just in front of the frustrated innkeeper. Giacomo dodges behind one particularly drunken dancer and pokes his foot under her skirt. This chase and Giacomo's antics amuse the crowd and Angelo is within striking distance when Giacomo suddenly throws the woman's skirts high in the air and disappears beneath them.

The drunken woman is oblivious to this and just keeps on twirling around the floor with a very sweaty and angry Angelo following her waiting for the dwarf to re-appear. In the meantime the Countess's hand moves further up Dante's thigh. He grabs a large glass of wine and almost downs it in one swallow, immediately refilling the glass.

Chapter 11

The following morning Angelo Nadalini sits in a much quieter kitchen smoking a long stemmed pipe and drinking coffee.

Several kitchen staff are quietly going about their tasks. The air of tranquility about the place is suddenly shattered as Dante crashes through a door leading from the main body of the inn. He stumbles across towards Angelo and drops into a chair opposite him.

He holds his head in both hands and lets out a quiet groan.

"Another successful evening then?"

Dante answers with a louder groan as Angelo pours out a strong coffee into a small cup and pushes it across to him. Dante takes a sniff at it, gags, groans again and pushes it away.

Angelo's smile widens.

"Very successful."

Dante peers through his fingers and asks, "My Violin, where is it?"

Angelo takes a moment or two before he casually answers.

"The dwarf's got it."

Dante sits upright.

"What?"

"He said he would look after it. After you collapsed, he took it to his room."

"His room? Which one is it?"

Dante begins to rise, slowly.

Again Angelo takes his time in answering. He leans across the table and grins lewdly at Dante.

"Same as yours. You shared with him."

He laughs and continues.

"You slept with him."

Dante is speechless and stares at Angelo as he continues, enjoying every moment.

"Made sense to me. When I finally caught him, I made a deal. Share his room with you or get out."

Dante sits down again.

Angelo is very amused.

"You didn't care; you were almost unconscious at the time. Should have worked out well for you, him being so small. I thought you would have more room in the bed."

The look of horror on Date's face makes him burst out laughing.

Dante is almost too hung over to take everything in and he struggles to think straight. Angelo milks the situation for his own pleasure.

"The dwarf seemed very happy with the arrangement."

The full implication of what Angelo is saying finally becomes clear and Dante almost throws up at the thought of it. He quickly rises and crosses to the door where he stops and turns.

"Where is he now?"

Nonchalantly, Angelo waves the long stem on his pipe to the outer door.

"Well on the way to Rome; they left hours ago."

Another shock for Dante and he leans against the wall as Angelo produces a small leather bag from his pocket.

"The Countess left this for you."

He tips the contents of the bag onto the table. A small coin rolls out and spins to a stop.

"There was more but I deducted the cost of the wine you ordered for everyone. You were very generous, Dante."

Again he leers at Dante.

"The Countess said you were a lovely boy, very talented, strong, virile."

Angelo draws out the last word and it has the desired effect as a very ashen Dante holds his hand over his mouth and dashes through the doorway.

With a satisfied smile on his face, Angelo picks up the coin and puts it into his pocket.

Chapter 12

The area around the Theatre Argentina in Rome is a warren of dark, narrow, cobbled alleyways which are lit only by the dim glow spilling from the many tavernas and squalid brothels. In spite of the unsavoury looking locale, there are numerous other coffee and drinking houses that attract the more gentrified clientele visiting the famous theatre.

It is in one of the more run down establishments at the rear of the theatre that an exhausted looking Dante is paying for a small drink. He counts his change and is astonished at the cost. He enviously watches some customers on a nearby table who are leisurely picking their way through a selection of dishes of hot food, and leaving some to be taken away back to the kitchen.

Sitting in a sweat stained shirt and with his hair sticking to his forehead, Dante presents a miserable sight which matches his mood. Suddenly, the stage doors burst open and a rush of silk clad and bewigged musicians pour out and frantically dash to the nearest bar.

Dante quickly puts down the cup and stands on his chair peering into the unruly and laughing crowd. He had enquired and been told that it was a dress rehearsal tonight and that this was his opportunity to finally catch up with Antonio.

He calls out Antonio's name but his words are drowned out by the noise of the musicians as they pass by in the alley. He cannot recognise any of them because of the wigs they are all wearing. Then, with a wild whoop, one of them pulls off his wig as he enters the Taverna. It is Antonio. Dante calls out his name and waves his hand, but Antonio doesn't see him; he shouts out his name again but the words have barely left his mouth when he is roughly pulled down from his chair and pushed up against the wall.

His assailant is also bewigged, but the man pulls it off with one hand as he holds Dante with the other. Raimundo Campese is very strong for a violinist and he has no trouble pinning Dante against the wall as he pulls back his right hand to punch him.

Realising what is about to happen, Dante reaches down and grabs Campese's crutch. Wasting no time, he squeezes, very hard. The result is instantaneous. Campese almost freezes to the spot as the pain from his crushed genitals reaches his brain. Within a second or two tears form in his eyes and he begins to buckle at the knees as he mumbles some unrecognizable words that are distorted by his agony.

Dante pulls the man upright and meets no resistance as he leans into his ear and whispers harshly, "I do not know what your problem is, but I do not want your aggression. In the past two days I have been beaten up, I have left my family, been robbed and possibly raped by a dwarf and molested by an aristocratic crone. I have also walked fifty miles."

He squeezes hard as Campese begins to slump against him and whimpers in pain.

Dante continues.

"I am tired, footsore and hungry. I did not touch your girl in the barn and if you did not get so drunk that she walked away from you then you would not be here with the future of your family in my fist. When I let you go just walk away and never come near me ever again. I am not good for you."

He very slowly releases his grip on Campese's crutch and the man lets out a sob of relief as he sits heavily on the stone floor.

The incident has attracted some onlookers who crowd round the two men. Antonio, noticing the crowd pushes his way through to the front.

He sees Raimundo on the floor.

"Raimundo, do get up. You will ruin those breeches and you know the maestro likes us to look like freshly scrubbed little boys all the time."

Campese just moans again, looks up, sees Antonio and murmurs under his breath.

"He is your friend, Antonio. You planned this."

It is at this point that a slightly bemused Antonio spots Dante who is almost standing beside him. He embraces him and pulls him to one side.

"Fiddler, I thought I might get to see you again. You have a streak of insanity running through you."

He nods in the direction of Campese.

"Give me a hand with him, would you?"

He moves to help his companion, but Campese is already getting to his feet.

With a look of hatred on his face, he points at Dante and says, "You will pay for this, country boy; you will pay dearly."

With that he pushes his way through the small crowd of gapers and hobbles off into the dimly lit alleyway.

Antonio watches him go and then puts his arm over Dante's shoulder.

"Well, it seems you made a lasting impression on him, fiddler. Well done!"

He smiles and slaps him on the back.

"Right, on with the evening. Home for a wash, change of clothes, get out of these stupid rags, then food, drink and women. What do you say?"

Without waiting for an answer, he continues, "Then you can tell me your story and from the look of you there must be one."

Still wrapping his arm around Dante's shoulder, Antonio sweeps him out and into the main square fronting the theatre.

Chapter 13

Two hours later both men are sitting in a pleasant and busy tavern; both are looking well groomed and Dante is wearing some of Antonio's clothes. Several empty bottles of wine are on the table in front of them and the remnants of a meal are being cleared away by a pretty and flirtatious young waitress.

Antonio manages to slide his hand under her wide skirt to have a secret feel of her bare thigh as she leans over the table in front of him to collect an empty dish. She giggles, then sees the owner looking at her and lightly slaps Antonio on the shoulder before she scuttles off, smiling to herself.

Dante leans forward.

"Did you touch her?"

Antonio smiles.

"Of course I did. Wouldn't want to disappoint her, would I?"

A shocked Dante whispers, "But this is a public place."

"That makes it even more fun, but not as much fun as your tale of woe, Dante. Going through all of that just to be here. Are you always so thorough at kicking yourself in the arse?"

Dante nods and gives a wry smile.

"And now I have to find that accursed dwarf to get my violin back. I hope he doesn't realise its worth. If he sells it then it will be lost forever. And I promised to look after it with my life."

Antonio laughs out loud.

"Well, that promise lasted a day! You might make a musician yet; you seem to have the requisite moral failings. But, I do know of this Countess. Mozart has many followers among the aristocracy, but this particular one has a reputation for liking entertainers."

He smiles slyly at Dante.

"As you are aware!"

He laughs again as Dante shakes his head and begins to redden.

"If she has made it to Rome, then I will get to hear of it."

He raises his glass.

"But first we have something more important to do."

"What could be more important?"

"Finding you some work. I cannot afford to keep a glutton like you, Dante. But in the meantime you would do well to learn the debauched ways of musicians and where better to do that than here in the eternal city."

The two men clink glasses and down the contents in one gulp.

Chapter 14

Antonio is a very experienced tutor in the pleasant art of debauchery and he is evenly matched in his enthusiasm for the seamier side of life by a still wide eyed and innocent Dante. There are many places in Rome where two young men who are hell bent on pleasure can find it and they enthusiastically lend themselves to the task.

Moving along the dark passageways they visit as many taverns as possible and are soon very drunk. An alcohol dazed Dante follows Antonio's example and when he grabs the well rounded bottom of a woman in a tavern, Dante does the same. The outraged woman's husband and his friends roughly throw them both out into the street.

As they sit in the gutter both of them start giggling. Antonio struggles to his feet exclaiming, "Right, my friend, enough for the night! Now it is time for bed."

He helps Dante up.

"Unlike you, fiddler, I have to pretend I know what I am doing tomorrow at rehearsals, so we must abandon our gentle slide into oblivion and make our way home."

They both look up and down the alley.

"Dante, have you any idea where we are?"

Dante can only shake his head.

"Which means we are completely lost because I don't know either."

Both men start to laugh and leaning against each other they weave their way into the gloom.

Chapter 15

The following day, as the sun is just beginning to slide behind the distant hills, Dante sits in the window of Antonio's very small room. He is reading some sheet music and humming to himself.

The furniture in the room is sparse and consists of a small, narrow bed, a set of drawers and wash stand, plus a large and battered armchair. Dante's clothes are neatly laid over the back of the chair and there is a bed sheet carefully folded on the floor below it.

A smaller window is the only other source of illumination, apart from two candlesticks placed on a small shelf. The candles are almost down to their holders and unlit.

Suddenly Antonio bursts through the door. As he enters he begins to take off his silk jacket shouting out to Dante, "She's here! Haven't seen her, but heard she visited the theatre sometime today."

Dante puts down the music on the bed.

"How do you know it's her?"

"I was told an old aristocrat had been visiting the Maestro. Had a dwarf with her; had a German or Austrian accent. Has to be her."

"Where is she now?"

Antonio pulls on another jacket and throws one to Dante.

"They were overheard saying they would be going over to Trastevere. C'mon, fiddler. Get that on and let's get over there."

Dante begins to put on Antonio's old jacket.

"Where is Trastevere?"

Antonio smiles at him.

"Trastevere is where angels fear to tread, Dante; a place only for souls that wish to be damned."

"Then why would the Countess, an aristocrat, a woman, want to go there?"

Antonio sits on the bed and looks intently at his roommate.

"Dante, sometimes you do surprise me. But that's what happens if you spend your youth on a farm in the middle of the country."

Dante is puzzled by this.

"Why, what do you mean? If this Trastevere is dangerous, then why would she go there?"

Antonio gets up and laughs as he walks to the door.

"It is dangerous, Dante, because it attracts perverts like the Countess. Lots of them. And, they are all seriously deranged people. They are not normal. The aristocracy invented perversions; they were the only ones with the time and money enough to indulge their fantasies. Trastevere is their feeding bowl. Now, will you please show some urgency. I wish to join them."

And with that, he steps out of the room; within a second Dante follows.

Chapter 16

Trastevere is in an ancient part of the city that has not changed much since Roman times. It is a warren of dark alleyways filled with taverns and brothels which display signs offering every manner of sexual diversion for the 'Discerning Gentleman'.

That the area is completely crowded by sightseers, rubberneckers or indeed, by discerning gentlemen, is no surprise.

It is into this crowded, badly lit and dangerous place that Antonio leads Dante.

They push and shove their way down the narrow walk ways and try to peer into the heavily curtained windows and doorways; all of the taverns have burly doormen in attendance. These men seem to take great pleasure in kicking out and pushing away any passersby who do not appear to have the financial where-withal to be a potential client, but if they see a likely looking couple or well-heeled and well-dressed men, then they rapidly clear a way through the crowd to enable them to walk through readily opened doors.

Dante and Antonio are given some leeway by the barkers and bouncers as they are not too shabbily dressed and they allow the pair to listen at the windows or doors for a few seconds before they move on.

After completing a search down one alley, they turn a corner into yet another one where the barkers are trying to outdo each other by describing, in lurid detail, the various sexual activities that are now being carried out in their fine salons. Dante is leading the way and suddenly stops; Antonio almost walks into him.

"What is it?" he asks, as Dante stands stock still and cups one hand behind his ear.

"There, can't you hear it?"
Antonio shakes his head.
"Hear what?"
"My violin, that tone. It's definitely a De-Munk."
Antonio listens intently as the sound of a violin, badly played, drifts down the crowded lane towards them.
"Sounds like a cat giving birth to me."
"Listen carefully. That is definitely a De Munk. *My* De Munk. Down here."
He begins to push pedestrians aside as he moves as fast as the crowd will allow, making his way to the source of the music. Within a few yards they both stop at the large doors of a slightly more salubrious looking salon than they had seen so far. Dante puts his ear to the door, but he is roughly pulled away by one of two very large men.
The man holds Dante by the shoulder of his jacket.
"What do you want?"
Dante pulls himself free.
"Is there a Countess in there?"
The two barkers look at each other, give a little smile, and then one of them leans close to Dante.
"Dozens of them! Is that what you like then? Countesses? Rich meat?"
The man who had stopped Dante puts his hand on the large brass door knob, as if to open it.
"We have black ones, white ones, yellow ones and if you have a particular shade in mind, we can paint one for you."
He smiles at Dante, adding, "Sir."
Antonio steps towards the door.
"A real one. Old and with a dwarf."
The barker raise his eyebrows and has a little think.
"Might have."
The second man moves to stand behind Antonio.
"Cost you to find out."
From the interior of the building there is a burst of violin music, a cackle of laughter and a roar of cheers.
Dante looks at Antonio.

"That's the violin and the dwarf."

He reaches into his pocket and pulls out his little leather purse.

"How much?"

Antonio pushes him and the two men away from the door and opens it.

"Nothing. Follow me."

Dante is slightly open mouthed and looks at the two men who shrug their shoulders as he hesitantly walks past them and follows Antonio into the brightly lit entrance.

The heavily gilded hallway is spacious and elegantly lit by numerous chandeliers. There are a number of doors leading off the marble floored reception area and Antonio moves swiftly along them, listening to each one, as he goes.

"Dante, you don't pay to come into places like this; the clients are the entertainment."

Antonio's words are falling on deaf ears. Dante is standing in the middle of the room and looking up the broad stairs that curve away to the upper floor. He is transfixed.

Walking slowly down the stairs is a beautiful young woman and she is smiling at Dante. Her long dark hair is draped over the smooth white skin of her shoulders.

She is completely naked.

As she reaches the bottom of the stairs she walks to one of the doors and opens it. Leaning against the door jamb and still looking at Dante, she puts a finger into her mouth, wets it, then slowly rubs it around one of her erect nipples.

Dante had never seen a fully grown naked adult female before, nor had he ever experienced an almost instant erection; until this moment.

Antonio turns and immediately notices the rising in Dante's tight breeches. So does the girl, who starts to giggle. Dante is completely mortified and begins to turn away and cover himself as Antonio walks over to him.

"What is it to be, Dante?"

He indicates the now helplessly laughing girl.

"A fuck or your fiddle?"

Dante is speechless.

Casting a glance at the girl, Antonio says, "You only have one fiddle!"

Still attempting to hide his now very obvious erection, Dante walks to the door where Antonio had been listening. Tossing a coin to the girl Antonio joins him and they both put their ears to the lacquered woodwork. As they listen there is a peal of laughter and a short burst of music from a fiddle. Dante nods at his companion and without waiting further they open the doors and stride into the room.

Over twenty people are crowded into the gilded salon. The only ones who are wearing clothes are the wine waiters who stand in each corner with trays of champagne.

No-one appears to be drinking much as the few bystanders are engrossed in watching a writhing mass of naked bodies on the floor; discarded clothes are piled up on chairs and sofas.

Limbs are intertwined; lips, hands and genitals are all being used as everyone seems intent on their own gratification; no-one notices the two newcomers.

There is a continuous buzz of voices and lots of laughter accompanied by the occasional groan or yelp. Dante is completely phased by this scene. He has never witnessed anything remotely like this in his life. So much naked flesh, so many naked buttocks, breasts, vaginas and erect penises on display, all in pursuit of the most enjoyable activity known to mankind. Unbridled and uninhibited sex.

Dante's mind is dizzy at the sight and the erection in his breeches stiffens further.

Antonio meanwhile is busy peering into the pile of bodies. After a moment, he turns to Dante.

"Can't see him. A dwarf, you say?"

Dante nods, still staring at the scene.

Antonio points at Dante's crutch.

"Keep that thing fettered Dante. This is by invitation only. No interlopers."

Dante nods again, then points at the pile.

"There."

Antonio turns to see a purple codpiece being thrust into the air. The owner is buried under some large naked female.

"I thought you said he was a small man."

"That's his codpiece; seems to wear it all the time."

Another burst of violin. Some laughter.

Dante frowns.

"That sounds like a De Munk, woefully out of tune tho'."

Antonio looks at him and shakes his head.

Dante points at the writhing mass.

"He is ruining it. How do we get it out of there?"

Antonio smiles, stands upright, thrusts back his shoulders and says, "There is only one way, fiddler. Follow me."

As he speaks the pile of bodies appears to part and Giacomo Grande emerges. He is sitting on the back of a large black man who seems to be having sex with the Countess who is spread-eagled beneath him. At each of the black man's thrusts, Giacomo plays a little note on the fiddle.

Seizing his chance, Antonio swiftly steps into the crowd, knocks Giacomo off his human steed and at the same time deftly grabs the violin which he throws to Dante; next to fly through the air is the bow, which Dante also catches.

This new diversion excites the crowd and they try to pull Antonio down among them. Before he disappears, he shouts to Dante, "Find the case. This is fun. Wait for me outside, I will only be a minute." He then sinks below a number of naked women who are desperately grabbing at his clothes.

Dante swiftly scours the room and finds the violin case in a corner. He carefully puts the violin away and somewhat hurriedly leaves the room.

The two barkers at the door eye Dante with some suspicion as he leaves the salon clutching the violin case. He stands a few feet away from them as he waits for Antonio whose breathless arrival is preceded by a bellow and lots of shouting from inside the building.

On hearing the noise, one of the barkers swings open the door as Antonio leaps through it and begins to pull Dante down the street.

"Hurry, Dante. I had to interlope a little to get what I wanted. They are not too pleased with me."

Both of them start to run as fast as their laughter will allow and turn the corner just as a small, sparsely dressed, crowd of angry men pour out of the salon into the street.

Chapter 17

A short time later Dante and Antonio noisily crash through the door to Antonio's room and both of them collapse onto the bed. They lie there trying to catch their breath between outbursts of loud laughter. Eventually, Dante gains enough control to be able to sit up, and carefully opens the violin case. Antonio peers over his shoulder.

"How is it?"

Dante is polishing the wood of the instrument with a handkerchief.

"Not too bad. Apart from one or two small scratches, it seems fine; the bow is a little raggy, though."

Antonio smiles as he falls back on the bed.

"Not surprised, considering where it's been recently. Not what it was crafted for."

They both start laughing again as Dante turns to him.

"Thank you, Antonio. I could never have done that. I am surprised that no-one tried to stop you."

Antonio leans against the pillow, his hands behind his head.

"That's the thing about orgies; you never know what will happen next."

"Yes. Well I wouldn't know about such things."

Patting Dante on the shoulder, Antonio sits up.

"All in the fullness of time, my friend. Oh, I almost forgot."

He reaches into the pocket of his jacket and hands a long purple codpiece to Dante.

"A little keepsake from your first one. Your little violin thief and bedmate is known as Giacomo Piccolo now."

Dante carefully picks up the codpiece using the handkerchief and waves it around as both of them laugh.

Antonio then pulls a red Cardinal's hat from his pocket and turns it inside out.

"The family crest says Cardinal Tomadini."

He places it on the bed post.

"I imagine there might be a very worried Cardinal in the morning, waiting for the blackmail note to arrive. Funny what your little friend had stuffed in his pockets."

He then turns.

"There something else I forgot to tell you."

The tone of Antonio's voice stops Dante in mid laugh.

"I have got you a job, Dante."

He immediately quells Dante's apparent enthusiasm. "Not as a musician, but you will be working very closely with Signor Mozart. You will have to start at the bottom. It is a very important job and there was a lot of competition for it; but, I used my influence."

Dante can't contain his excitement.

"What is it?"

"Tomorrow you will come to the theatre with me. It is the last dress rehearsal before the concert tomorrow night. I will introduce you to the great man and then you are on your own."

He smiles, almost to himself.

"All will be revealed then."

Dante can barely believe his good fortune and begins to furiously polish the violin. Antonio waits until his attention is fully diverted and then reaches into his jacket pocket. He takes a quick drink from the neck of the small green bottle before slipping it away again.

Chapter 18

In a large ornately decorated room just off the main entrance to the Theatre Argentina the diminutive figure of the young Mozart is surrounded by a small army of attendants who are fussing over every aspect of his appearance.

The composer is dressed in a pink silk suit with a purple velvet jacket. A valet is carefully adjusting a cravat when the large doors open and a flunky enters to announce the arrival of the Pope's emissary for his audience with the Maestro.

There is a flurry of activity as finishing touches are applied. When it is deemed that no more can be done to enhance sartorial perfection, the attendants stand back to admire their efforts and then the young man sees a very nervous Dante in the corner of the room and walks over to him.

Without actually making eye contact with Dante, Mozart addresses him.

"I suppose we had better do it now. I really don't know how long this Cardinal will take. They are usually long winded, think they must always give a sermon."

Mozart stands in front of Dante and holds his arms out on either side. Moments pass. Dante has no idea what he is expected to do.

Mozart almost whispers to him, "Come along, can't wait all day."

He still stands with his arms akimbo, then whispers again, "The pot. Get the pot."

Then he looks at his attendants.

"The important thing is there should be no stains. Silk takes forever to dry and you can always tell."

Dante is now in a panic. Everyone in the room is looking at him. He turns and then sees a chamber pot on the small chest behind him. He picks it up by the handle. There is a small cloth draped over its side. He turns back to Mozart who is now looking at him with a frown on his face as he nods once again in the direction of his crotch.

The dreadful truth dawns on Dante and he moves as if in a trance.

Kneeling down in front of the composer, he undoes the small buttons on the fly of the breeches and then stops. With a snort of annoyance Mozart reaches in and proceeds to point his penis into the chamber pot that Dante is still holding. When the flow has stopped to Mozart's satisfaction, he utters one word.

"Wipe."

Dante, still in a state of shock, does exactly that.

Another command.

"Fasten."

With trembling hands, Dante does up the fly buttons. When he is finished and without another word Mozart turns on his heels and marches out of the room, followed by his entire entourage.

Dante is alone, the chamber pot and its contents are on the marble floor and the wiping cloth is still in his hands. He looks at the pot, then at the cloth. Realising what it is, he drops it like a hot coal and then looks up at the ceiling as he screams out at the top of his voice.

"Antonio!"

He starts to rub his hands as if they were burning. He picks up the pot and drops the cloth into it. Moving to an open window overlooking an alleyway, he empties the contents and in a moment of self-disgust drops the chamber pot into the alley.

Looking up at the sky, he angrily shouts out once again, "Antonio! I will get you for this."

At the very same time, Antonio and the entire string section of the orchestra are making their way along the alley to the stage door, some three floors below Dante.

On hearing his name being shouted , Antonio looks up and is just in time to dodge a flying chamber pot and its contents.

The man directly behind him, Raimundo Campese, is not so lucky and the pot hits him directly on the head smashing as it does so. Campese immediately falls to the ground as Antonio looks up and stares into the terrified face of Dante.

Chapter 19

Dante paces up and down the ante room. Antonio is sprawled in a chair and finds it difficult to contain his laughter. Dante keeps giving him dark looks as he walks by.

"The trouble with you, fiddler, is that you have no discernible sense of humour."

A very depressed Dante almost mumbles to himself.

"The nearest I have got to being in an orchestra is holding a piss pot for a composer."

He stops and points a finger at Antonio.

"And it's your fault. You knew what the job was; you led me on."

Still laughing, Antonio sits up on the chair.

"Fiddler, I told you that you would not get a job in Mozart's orchestra. There is a waiting list of hundreds of trained musicians. Why would he ever take on a farm boy? I did say you would start at the bottom. You just never listen."

Dante continues with his pacing.

"But a piss pot!"

"At least you got near one of the most popular composers in the world. Count yourself lucky. It was certainly lucky for me."

Dante stops mid pace and looks at him.

"Lucky? How?"

"It got me the job as second violinist. Battle-field promotion. The first violinist had really no choice; we play in a few minutes."

For the first time Dante is contrite.

"How bad is the cut?"

Antonio smiles.

"Unfortunately, not too bad; but, it will keep him out of this concert."

As he finishes speaking, a little bell sounds outside the room.

"Five minutes. Time to get nervous."

Antonio stands and adjusts his clothes; then, he takes a little green bottle from his pocket, takes a quick swig and makes for the door.

Dante stops him.

"Antonio, what am I going to do? No job and almost no money."

Antonio looks at the now almost distraught younger man. He reaches into his jacket pocket and pulls out an envelope.

"You could always come with me, do some training on the job so to speak."

Dante is puzzled.

"What?"

Waving the envelope in Dante's face, Antonio smiles. This was waiting for me this morning when I arrived here. Appointment to be first violinist for a series of concerts in Venice starting in a week's time. But I don't have a third violinist."

He taps the envelope on his teeth.

"Don't suppose you would want the job? Not a big orchestra, just a quartet playing to drunken socialites and rich merchants in a waterlogged northern shithole."

Dante is furiously nodding his head as Antonio carries on speaking.

"For virtually no money; rat infested garrets to sleep in."

Dante butts in.

"Yes, yes I would! But why are you leaving Mozart's orchestra?"

Antonio's answer leaves Dante completely lost for words.

"Because this is the last concert for a while and it also suits my purpose right now. We leave tomorrow. Must dash, got a Pope waiting! See you later."

Antonio briskly turns and leaves the room as Dante slowly realises what he has just said. He jumps up and down, spins around the room, then sinks into the chair. After a few moments he drops to his knees, crosses himself and begins to pray.

Chapter 20

Exactly one week later, a sumptuous party is taking place on the terrace of a large Palazzo which overlooks the Grand Canal.

Servants wait with trays of food and drinks as the extravagantly dressed guests alight from their gondolas on the private jetty that leads up to the brightly lit entrance to the Palazzo. Everyone is in high spirits and party mood.

Three men quietly sip drinks on a small balcony that overlooks the main room. They are not as opulently dressed as the rest of the guests and watch idly as the assorted Venetian gentry make merry just fifteen feet below them.

It is Antonio who points to a man in a purple silk suit making his way through the crowd to stop beside a large bellied man sporting a very tall yellow wig and to whisper in his ear. The fat man nods and the one in the purple suit looks up to the balcony and waves.

Antonio turns to his two companions, Dante and a rather thin man about the same age as Antonio who is nonchalantly holding a cello.

"Shit, they want us to start playing now!"

He looks around the room below.

"Where the hell is she?"

Lorenzo, the cello player looks sharply at Antonio.

"She is always late. I don't know why you still use her."

Antonio picks up his violin and gives a half smile.

"Three reasons: one, she is talented…."

He looks at Lorenzo who nods slightly.

"…..two, she is beautiful, and the third reason is…."

Lorenzo butts in sharply and finishes the sentence for him.

"…..and three, she can wrap you around her little finger! Right?"

Antonio just laughs to himself as Dante asks, "Who?"

"Luisa Bazzo," is Lorenzo's reply.

Dante is no wiser and looks to Antonio for an answer.

"She is a second violinist, one of the original Virgins of Venice."

He carries on, ignoring Lorenzo's little snort.

"In name only, of course."

Dante is still no wiser and merely shrugs as Antonio motions them to their chairs. He places a sheaf of music sheets on his stand and flicks through them.

"We shall have to start with the Concerto for 2 Violins in A major."

He grins at Dante.

"By your favourite, Signor Vivaldi. Are you up to this, fiddler? Bit of a solo in the middle; it's all yours."

A slightly flustered Dante is hurriedly leafing through his sheet music.

"We haven't practiced this. I hardly know it."

Antonio winks at Lorenzo.

"These clods wouldn't realise even if we didn't play it."

He taps Dante on the shoulder with his bow.

"If you have a problem, then improvise."

Antonio leads off and Dante follows him. The guests on the floor below them applaud politely as the sound of the music reaches them. They simply ignore the musicians and carry on chatting as more food and drink is served.

The two musicians are not concerned about the audience either and are simply enjoying playing. Lorenzo is turning the music for Dante and Antonio is playing from memory. Lorenzo turns another page and taps at the sheet where the solo begins. Antonio grins manically at Dante who is now sweating and suffering a mild panic attack.

The solo moment arrives and Dante prepares to hit the first note when from behind him a violin begins to play the solo piece.

The three men turn.

Luisa Bazzo is a stunning twenty something brunette; she is wearing a black velvet dress that highlights the sheen on her slightly tanned shoulders. She smiles at them as she effortlessly plays the solo. Dante is immediately smitten by her beauty and just stares at her. This is the most beautiful woman he has ever seen.

The solo section is almost over and Luisa nods at Dante. Hurriedly he puts his violin in place and the pair of them begin the final part which is a return to the duet.

In perfect synchronisation, the violinists' fingers move frantically on the strings of their instruments as they reach the climax. The audience politely applaud. None of the musicians notice.

Chapter 21

Some hours later in the quiet back room of a small tavern that faces out onto a narrow canal, the string quartet are nearing the end of their fourth bottle of wine and are a bit worse for wear.

As their meal dishes are cleared away, Antonio orders another bottle. A slightly tipsy Luisa manages to rise to her feet and puts some coins on the table.

"Enough for me, gentlemen. I must retire to my princess castle before they raise the drawbridge."

The three men immediately protest at her leaving and plead with her to stay. Luisa smiles at them all in turn then in a slightly sarcastic way she looks straight at Antonio.

"It has been a wonderful evening in the company of three delightful men, but as you know Antonio I only do it for the money."

She smiles sweetly at him and he returns the compliment as she continues.

"This must be the first time you have ever paid me at the end of a performance, any performance."

She casts a brief look at Dante before turning back.

"It must be your influence, Dante."

She wags a finger in Antonio's face.

"Careful, he might just make a human being out of you!"

Without another word she quickly walks away from the table and disappears into the night. The three men watch her go and a slight silence descends.

Still wearing his smile, Antonio finally speaks.

"Bitch."

Slightly shocked by the venom in Antonio's voice, Dante turns to him.

"She is beautiful, and talented. Why do you have to say that?"

Lorenzo quickly answers.

"A long story but an interes….."

He is abruptly silenced by a suddenly angry Antonio.

"A very long and a very tedious story. I am sure we don't need to bore Dante with it."

He gives Lorenzo a hard stare.

"Do we?"

A dark mood settles on the trio. Dante and Lorenzo share a quick glance; Antonio seems lost in thought and stares at the floor. Suddenly he rises and addresses the other men.

"Come on, you two. You look as damp as this watery dump. There must be something exciting happening here. We are young, handsome, rampant and we have money, so let's go and find it."

Throwing a few coins on the table, he suddenly sweeps out of the room and out of the tavern, leaving his companions to scramble after him.

Chapter 22

The sun has not yet risen but the sky has a pink glow to it and silhouettes a pair of pigeons sitting on the narrow window sill of a shabby run down villa in a seedy area of Venice that begin to copulate. The noise from the flapping of the birds' wings wakes one of the occupants of the room inside.

Lorenzo opens his eyes, spots the birds and reaches out to find something to throw at them; his wildly groping hand falls upon the naked and full breast of the girl lying next to him on a straw mattress. Almost still asleep the girl giggles and turns over. Lorenzo follows her and begins to caress her. She giggles some more as he leans over and begins to nibble her ear. That is when he spots the four naked bodies on two other mattresses on the floor.

The room is littered with empty wine bottles and some plates of leftover food. He releases the girl's breast, finds a gnawed bone on the floor and throws it at the window. This scares the birds and they take off in a noisy flurry of feathers.

Lorenzo whispers to the girl to stop giggling but it is too late. Antonio blinks, looks around and then folds himself into the girl beside him. He immediately goes back to sleep.

Dante's companion has long blonde hair which is tied up at the back of her head. She watches the other two couples and then undoes her hair; carefully rising to her knees, she drapes her hair over his face.

It takes a few moments of this to make Dante aware of the irritation and he drowsily brushes it away. She laughs and throws one of her legs over his body to sit astride him. This has the desired effect and Dante is suddenly wide awake. He stares at the girl as if he had never seen her before then slowly places his hands on her hips. She rises and then settles down again, all of this without a word being spoken.

The copulating pigeons return to their perch on the window ledge.

Chapter 23

Two large women are being helped into a gondola at one of the many landing places on the main canal.

They are being watched with amusement by Lorenzo and Dante who are leaning on a balustrade opposite. They both laugh at the performance of the gondolier who is taking advantage of the women's unsteadiness as they clamber aboard the rocking gondola. He runs his hands over their bodies in the guise of assisting them. Neither of the two women seem to object and smile coyly to each other as they settle down on the cushioned seat.

"She is beautiful."

Lorenzo looks at Dante and then back to the women in the boat.

"Which one?"

"What?"

"They are both fat and ugly! That boatman is welcome to them."

Lorenzo nods in the direction of the gondola.

Dante laughs.

"Not them! Luisa!"

Now Lorenzo has a little laugh as he considers his reply.

"She is. But she is also poison."

Dante ignores this remark as he turns to look at him.

"But she plays so well. Like an angel."

"Got to give you that one, Dante."

He smiles to himself.

"She should. She was trained by your hero; well almost."

They both begin to walk along the canal side.

"What do you mean?"

"Vivaldi. He was her tutor. Or would have been if he had lived long enough."

Dante stops dead in his tracks as Lorenzo casually walks on.

"What?!"

Lorenzo puts a hand on Dante's shoulder.

"She was placed in a convent as a child. Her father thought she was surplus to family requirements and did not want to pay a dowry. He only wanted boys apparently."

Dante slowly takes this in.

"And you say she was influenced by the maestro?"

They both begin to walk again. Lorenzo smiles.

"That's why Antonio thinks she hates all men. Getting some form of revenge on her father."

Once again Dante stops Lorenzo and gently pushes him against a canal side balustrade.

"Stop talking in riddles. How? Vivaldi was dead before she was born and why would he play in a nunnery.?"

Lorenzo shrugs his shoulders.

"Who knows? His devotion to the faith maybe; perhaps his desire to awaken a musical appreciation in those about to devote their lives in the service of their God......Anyway after his death, some of his devoted and talented orchestra members continued in his footsteps. Maybe they just did it for that other old thing.....money! She would have been heavily influenced by him."

"Money? From nuns?"

Dante can't believe what he is hearing.

"How remote is your farm, Dante? Of course, money. Girls like Luisa are ostensibly being trained to become nuns, but most of them come from rich families who happily pay large amounts to have them taken off their hands."

A puzzled Dante shakes his head.

"Luisa is a nun?"

"Absolutely not. Antonio's story is that she broke out. Literally, made a hole in the convent wall. Took a while; she had to do it brick by brick. In the meantime, she learned to play the violin. Then when she could squeeze through the hole, she simply left."

"What did she do then?"

Lorenzo turns to look out over the canal.

"Not a lot. She stayed in Venice, played at parties and in taverns. She was building a reputation and was making a living; then, she had a stroke of great misfortune."

"What happened to her?"

Lorenzo leans on the stone wall. "Antonio arrived back in town."

Lorenzo lets this sink in, casts a quick glance at Dante and then continues.

"She was completely besotted by him. I suppose you could say she loved him, not that he noticed. They were together for about a year."

"He didn't love her?"

"Antonio… love anyone… other than himself?"

He laughs as he shakes his head.

"He says he met her at a soiree, heard her play, offered to take her under his wing as long as she agreed to get under his blanket. He recognised her talent and wanted to use it as an asset for himself; he also saw her as a beautiful body, which he also wanted to use for himself."

As Dante listened, he absent mindedly stares at a couple of gondolas as they slide past on the oily water of the canal.

"Why did they part?"

"Antonio got bored. He does that with women. He went back to his usual tricks: whoring and his beloved opium."

"Opium?"

Lorenzo nods.

"He is an addict."

He falls silent as he remembers what happened.

"She had her suspicions. Missing money, staying away, little things like that. But the last straw was finding him in her bed with two whores, all completely stupefied. She walked out and never went back."

Dante stands behind Lorenzo.

"Where does she live?"

"You really don't want to know. Let her go, Dante. She is damaged property."

"Tell me."

Shrugging his shoulders, he reluctantly gives in.

"She lives in a small place behind her former convent. Santa Maria delle Vergini."

He turns and points.

"On that little island over there. But you really are wasting your ti…."

He stops when he realises he is talking to himself and sees Dante sprinting along the walkway in the direction of the bridge leading to the island.

Chapter 24

Dante is slightly out of breath as he climbs the last of the narrow stone stairs to the top of the building. There is only one door on the small landing. The dirt pitted skylight lets in just enough light for him to see there is no name on the door.

Taking a small handkerchief from his pocket, he wipes his sweaty brow, runs his fingers through his hair and adjusts his clothes. Standing as tall as he can he prepares to knock on the door, then hesitates, runs his fingers through his hair again, adjusts his clothing once more, takes a deep breath and knocks firmly.

He waits.

Nothing happens. He knocks again, this time with a little more gusto. Again there is no response. He carefully puts his ear to the door and listens. After a few moments it is obvious that no-one is home.

Dante starts down the stairs again but pauses as he hears someone slowly climbing upwards. He stands still and waits. A girl's head appears. In the dim light Dante doesn't recognise her. She stops when she sees him. After a moment or two of mutual peering, she looks down the stairs behind her.

"There's someone here. Did you order him?" she whispers loudly.

Another face appears.

"No, I didn't order him, but I do know who he is."

Dante recognises Luisa's voice.

The two girls continue to watch Dante through the curving stair rails. He smiles as Luisa climbs the last few steps up to the top floor with her friend close behind her. They both move, rather unsteadily, to stand in front of the door. It is obvious that they are slightly tipsy and struggle to stop giggling.

Eventually Luisa calms down enough to attempt an introduction to the now slightly embarrassed Dante.

"Dante Gabriele, allow me to introduce my very good friend Lara who is also a music student."

The two of them shake hands as Lara once again bursts out laughing. Luisa turns to open the door of the room and firmly pushes her inside. She then turns back to Dante.

"If you are delivering a message from your best friend Antonio, the answer is still 'no'."

This slightly puzzles Dante.

"No. I have no message. I just wanted to talk to you about Signor Vivaldi's tutors. He is a great hero of mine."

Luisa opens the door and steps inside the room, holding the door between herself and Dante.

"Really? Well, it will have to wait for another time."

Lara joins her and tugs at her sleeve.

"As you can see, I am rather busy right now. I am sure we will have an opportunity to discuss music at a later date."

With that she firmly closes the door.

A very disappointed Dante stares at the door and after a moment or two makes his way carefully down the gloomy stairs.

Chapter 25

Early the following morning Dante visits the Chapel of Santa Maria and takes a seat in a rear pew. The weak sun fights the early morning mists that rise from the canal and filters through the half open door of this ancient church.

Dante has some difficulty in seeing what he has written on a long piece of parchment and he edges along the pew to get more light onto the yellow sheet.

The Chapel, even at this early hour, has a number of devotees all seated at the front near the altar rails. A low murmur of prayer is all that Dante can hear but even that is dismissed by him as he concentrates on re-reading his letter.

A slight blush reddens his face as he reads the lies that he is writing to his family, mainly about his wellbeing and his progress in the world of music; how he is making reasonable money by playing in the most sought after string quartet in the city; the size of his spacious lodgings and that he has met the most beautiful and talented woman on God's earth, after his mother of course.

When he has finished reading it for the third time, he slowly signs his name with a stubby little pencil and folds the document. He ties it with a short piece of silken ribbon and flattens it out on the bench. Clutching the letter to his chest, he quietly walks down the side aisle to the front and knocks on a small door beside the altar. There is no reply. He knocks again. Still no answer.

The worshippers now begin to take notice of him and one or two look at him as he places his ear to the door. From within he can hear the faint sounds of someone snoring and he slowly opens the door.

In the far corner of the stuffy room which is in almost total darkness, lies a priest, already adorned in the robes for taking Mass. He is asleep and snoring contentedly.

Dante closes the door and moves towards him.

"Father."

The priest continues snoring so Dante tries once more, slightly louder.

"Father."

The priest grunts and stops snoring. There is a short silence and without making any movement, not even opening his eyes, he speaks.

"What?"

"I have a letter, Father." Dante quickly adds, "For a Priest."

The priest opens one eye.

"Are you ordained in the faith?"

"No, Father, but this letter is to my uncle Emanuele, to pass on to my parents."

Still not moving but with one eye open, the priest mumbles.

"Which parish?"

"Ebosta, south of Rome."

There is a long moment of silence. The Priest slowly opens his other eye but remains motionless.

"Is this Priest named Gabriele?"

A surprised Dante nods.

"Yes."

The priest smiles.

"So that's where he finished up. Ebosta. The parish no-one will take. They didn't have a Priest there for years."

Closing one eye he moves for the first time. He raises his arm and points to a small table beside the door.

"Put it on there."

Dante carefully places his letter on the table and begins to open the door.

"Thank you, Father. How long will it take to get there?"

"The Lord's eternity if you don't leave money for the seal."

Dante moves back to the table as he digs some small coins from his pocket. He places half of them on the envelope. Again, without looking or moving, the Priest addresses him.

"To get beyond Rome it will need a large seal. His Holiness does not provide this holy service for nothing."

With only a moment's hesitation Dante quickly puts the rest of his coins on the table. The priest listens for a moment and then waves him out of the room. Once the door is closed he sits up and looks at the money. A slight sliver of daylight reveals his very fat and sweaty face.

He smiles and chuckles to himself.

"For that amount, I could deliver it myself."

Chapter 26

The rain pours through a tear in the canvas awning at the entrance to a shabby tavern down a dimly lit alley leading to the Grand Canal.

Dante huddles closer to the wall to avoid the spray.

The alley is home to a number of similar establishments that appear to cater for the lower paid citizens of Venice and they begin to arrive in groups of twos and threes, all skirting the small overflowing channel that runs down the middle of the narrow passage. In their haste to get out of the rain some of the hungry, thirsty customers bump into Dante. He holds his ground mainly because he has little choice; his back is up against the roughly hewn granite wall.

More workers begin to arrive and the alley becomes busy with customers. Peering through the shadowy jostling crowd, Dante eventually spies the person he has been waiting for.

Lorenzo sweeps around the top corner of the alley. He is wearing a long waterproof cloak and he uses this to shelter both himself and a girl who is clinging on to his waist. Both of them are laughing and in high spirits. When they pass Dante, he reaches out and grabs Lorenzo by the arm just as they are about to enter the warmly lit osteria.

Lorenzo swiftly turns to see who is holding him and then smiles.

"Dante, you startled me. Where have you been all day?"

He looks at the girl who he motions inside. She moves out from under his cloak and disappears through the door.

"We were waiting for you. It could have been an interesting afternoon."

He nods in the direction the girl had taken.

Dante smiles apologetically.

"I'm sorry. I had to send a letter to my family. I promised to write to them regularly. It took me a while to find the priest who does that."

Lorenzo steps into the shallow doorway as he begins to unwrap his cloak.

"You should have asked me. The fat old priest who runs the Chapel of Santa Maria, right?"

Dante is slightly taken aback.

"How did you know? It is supposed to be for priests only."

Lorenzo shakes his head and gives a little laugh.

"Don't be a fool. That fat old pervert would deliver a letter from the devil to a courtesan if the seal money was right. How much did you pay him?"

Pushing his hands deep into his pockets, Dante half smiles.

"Too much, I fear. All I had."

Lorenzo gives him a pitying look.

"Then you really are the fool. That friar will be as drunk as the devil by now. Probably trying to buy the services of some little choirboy for the night."

He places a hand on Dante's shoulder.

"Come on in, join us. I will treat you. Say hello to Maria, a sweet girl. You will really like her."

He nudges Dante with his elbow as he turns to enter the osteria.

"And I need a rest."

"Yes, I am sure she is good company, but tonight I am not. Could you loan me the price of a meal?"

Lorenzo looks at him and pulls some coins from his pocket. As he hands them over, he leans close to Dante.

"Don't waste your time on her; she is not good for you."

Dante is already moving away as he replies.

"Who?"

"Luisa. Who else?"

Dante shrugs his shoulders and feigns surprise as Lorenzo continues.

"Who I have just seen going into the Taverna D'Asti."

He indicates that it is around the corner .

Without saying another word Dante runs down the wet alleyway, heedless of the large puddles he splashes through.

Lorenzo watches him go murmuring to himself, "But she wasn't alone."

He watches until Dante turns the corner before entering the osteria.

Chapter 27

The Taverna D'Asti is busy. The bustling crowd waiting to get inside this popular tavern are standing under a large awning; waiters are busily pushing through them with laden trays of drink and food.

It is the beginning of Carnevale in Venice and most of the clientele are wearing elaborate costumes and colourful masks. Dante tries to squeeze through them but the crowd is too dense.

He desperately scans the faces of the women. Luisa is not among them. A waiter passes by with a full tray and Dante tugs at his arm to stop him.

"Luisa Bazzo. Is she here, inside?"

The waiter is less than happy at being held and he gently tries to pull himself free. The drinks on the tray start to wobble slightly.

"I don't know. It's crowded in there."

"Has she been here?"

The waiter is impatient now.

"Yes, earlier."

"Did you see her leave?"

"No. Now get off me. I'm busy."

Dante tugs at his sleeve again. The glasses begin to wobble.

"Did she leave?"

"Could have done. They were both wearing masks. Might have been her."

Dante is now becoming slightly desperate.

"Who was she with?"

The waiter finally frees his sleeve and begins to push through the crowd.

"A man, a very tall man; a musician."

Dante shouts at him as he disappears into the melee.

"How do you know he was a musician?"

The waiter is now completely absorbed by the crowd and Dante strains to hear his voice.

"He had a violin case over his shoulder and he had long blonde hair. Heard them talking about going to the Palazzo Augustin."

Dante steps back out of the shelter of the awning and stands in the rain for a second or two to absorb the information; he then turns on his heel and runs down the street.

Chapter 28

There are a number of routes to the Palazzo Augustine, one from the Grand Canal, accessible only by gondola, another from the slightly broader cobbled alley that leads to the wide gated entrance, and several other service alleyways which are used by the delivery men with their narrow barrows laden with materials for the Palazzo.

During the day these narrow passageways are bustling and to avoid being trampled by a speeding barrow man there are niches cut into the stone wall for pedestrians to jump into until the barrow passes by. At night they are silent and rarely used. When it is pouring down, they are never used.

Dante runs through the heavy rain, oblivious of his saturated state and the large pools of water which he splashes through. His anxiety and desperation to catch up with Luisa has blinded him to his own situation and also his safety. So much so that when he passes the end of one of the little narrow alleyways he stops, peers into the darkness and decides to take a chance. His shortcut will save him some precious seconds. He begins to sprint into the darkness.

He is not alone. When he is almost at the end of the narrow passageway, a large dark figure suddenly steps out from one of the stone niches and blocks his path. Without saying a word the man lunges at him. Dante manages to avoid the man's groping fingers and slams against the rain sodden wall; he turns to run back as the man tries once again to grab him. As Dante retraces his steps another figure steps around the far corner. This man is smaller than the one now lumbering after Dante and even in the very dim and misty glow from a distant street light Dante can see the glint of a stiletto dagger. He is trapped.

Standing with his back to the dripping wall he looks from one man to the other as they slowly close in on him.

"I have no money, no jewels, nothing!"

The big man gives a little laugh.

"You must have something. What do you think, Renzo?"

Renzo, the smaller man, twiddles the dagger in front of his face.

"Fausto, as we well know, everybody has something."

Dante now realises he is in serious danger and the slight tremor in his voice reveals his fear.

"I give you my word. I have absolutely nothing."

The two men slowly move in on their prey. Renzo suddenly strikes the wall with his blade, startling Dante. He scrapes it along the stone wall and it makes a screeching noise.

"You look well to do to me."

Fausto is now just a few feet away and moving very slowly towards Dante.

"Best we just take a little look, a little feel, see what is hidden under that fine shirt and jacket. See what is in those pants."

Renzo takes up the theme.

"See what I mean. Everybody has something that somebody else might take a fancy to. Might even be a body part or two. Those doctors like a little bit of meat to slice up, eh Fausto?"

Dante is now desperate. He knows he cannot escape these two men, who seem intent on causing him physical harm at the very least. The one called Fausto is now close enough for him to make out his features. He is grinning as he edges even closer.

Dante makes one last plea.

"Have you ever known a street musician to have any money? We play for our suppers and I am on my way to play for mine. I will share what I get, I promise."

This has no effect on the advancing duo and now they are within grabbing distance.

Then, a loud booming voice echoes down the alleyway.

"Did I hear the sound of a musician in distress?"

All three of them turn to see a very tall man dressed in a cloak and pointed hat standing at the end of the alley behind Renzo. The man appears to be about eight feet tall and even dwarfs Dante's attacker. The voice booms again, now louder and very angry.

"Well, did I? Answer me."

The three men are almost transfixed as they look at this giant who begins to stride along the alley towards them.

Dante seizes his chance and pushes at Fausto who suddenly produces a knife and slashes it in front of him. The razor sharp blade cuts across the back of Dante's hand and he falls to the floor, partly in shock at the sharp pain but also to avoid the second parry which swings just above his head.

Both robbers hesitate for a moment, take a quick look at the approaching giant and decide to remove themselves. They leap over Dante's body and run as fast as they can to the opposite end of the alley. The giant arrives and stands over Dante who is getting up from the floor.

"Couple of cowards, usually takes more than that to scare them away. Shouldn't hang about though, Dante. They might find their cojones and come back for yours."

Dante is surprised to hear the man use his name, but he is so relieved at his narrow escape he runs behind him as they quickly move back up the alleyway out into the open where there are a few passersby. They move across to where there is a small oil lamp burning in a wall niche. The man looks down at Dante; his face is covered by an ornate designed mask.

"Silly boy, Dante. Going down places like that. Not everyone likes you as much as I do."

The voice is slightly distorted by the mask, but Dante feels he knows it.

"Who are you? How do you know my name?"

Still towering over Dante the man laughs.

"Surely you must recognise me, Dante. After all the intimate moments we have shared together. Here, take a closer look."

The man's masked face suddenly disappears. The tall hat falls down onto his shoulders. The head also disappears. Dante is surprised by what is happening and keeps staring up when he feels a tug at his belt.

"Down here, Dante."

He looks down to be faced with the grinning face of Giacomo Grande.

"It's your old friend Giacomo."

Dante takes a step back in surprise. How can this be happening to him? First the robbers and now this.

"I knew you'd be pleased to see me; knew you would be searching for me, because you have something of mine that you want to return to me, haven't you?"

A puzzled Dante shakes his head.

"Have I?"

At that moment the big man begins to collapse. Giacomo deftly catches it as the cloak begins to envelop them both. He pulls it aside to reveal a pair of stilts which he gently lays on the floor and turns back to Dante, still smiling.

"I knew you were taken with it the moment you saw it."

A still puzzled Dante insists.

"What are you talking about?"

Giacomo gently prods him in the stomach.

"The thing you stole from me, remember?"

"No, I don't. I have no idea what you are talking about, but I must be off now. Thank you for helping me back there."

"Dante. I didn't just help you back there."

He leans closer.

"I saved your life. If I had not been passing by at that moment, your dead body would be lying, bleeding, in that gutter, and it would be naked. They would have killed you and stripped you of everything. You would just have been another dead body. You owe me your life, Dante."

This information is quite a shock to Dante and he leans against the wall. Giacomo moves even closer.

"Let me refresh your memory about the thing you stole from me."

He begins to stroke his codpiece in a masturbatory fashion. Dante steps quickly away from him.

Giacomo leers at him.

"Remember now?"

Dante nods.

"Your Codpiece?"

"Yes, Dante. A codpiece, but a very special one."

"But you can buy one of those anywhere."

Giacomo nods as he continues stroking.

"But not quite like that one. Have you still got it?"

Dante rubs at his forehead.

"Probably. I don't really know."

Giacomo's mood changes instantly. He grabs Dante by his belt and thrusts a stiletto between his thighs.

"Maybe this will refresh your memory, because if it doesn't then you will be missing *your* codpiece. Your real one."

"I am sure we still have it, back at the lodgings."

"Good. Take me there now."

Dante takes a chance.

"Please, Giacomo. First I must get to the Palazzo Augustine. Then I will take you to the lodgings. This is very important to me. Please."

Giacomo still keeps the pressure on the stiletto blade.

"What are you doing at the Palazzo?"

"There is someone there that I must talk to. It means a lot to me."

Giacomo takes a moment or two to consider this and then swiftly withdraws the blade. He points with it to the stilts and cloak.

"Bring him and follow me."

With that he runs as fast as he can along the alley, followed after a moment by Dante carrying the cloak clad stilts and pointed hat.

Chapter 29

Gondolas are mooring up at the canal side of the Palazzo Augustine and disgorging elegantly and exotically dressed guests onto the covered terrace. Giacomo and Dante watch from a covered awning opposite the front gateway where even more guests scurry to get inside out of the rain.

The sound of music floats across the small cobbled square as Giacomo turns to look at his very bedraggled and wet companion.

"This is a very high class affair, Dante. Have you been invited?"

Dante shakes his head.

"No. My friend is playing there."

Giacomo smiles thinly.

"Your friend who stole my codpiece and violin? "

Dante gives a little laugh.

"Retrieved my violin, you mean?"

Giacomo ignores him and carries on.

"During my finest hour, when I was completely distracted, reaching the climax of my performance."

"You were in the middle of an orgy."

Giacomo drops the smile and snaps back at him.

"I am an entertainer; I entertain people. It is what I do."

"No."

"No, what?"

"It is not *that* friend."

"Good. In that case, I will get you inside, invited or not. I am very interested to find out who this special friend is."

Chapter 30

Giacomo, in his 'tall man' outfit, strides purposefully across the driveway to the Palazzo. The ushers obviously realise that he must be part of the entertainment and wave him through the large open doorway.

Inside the Palazzo, Giacomo turns down the least occupied hallway and stops in a dark corner. Dante opens the bottom of the cloak and steps out. Giacomo slides down the stilts and joins him, sniggering.

"Not the first time you have been between my legs!"

Dante turns away from him in disgust as Giacomo carries on.

"Don't worry! It was just as innocent."

He leers at Dante.

"Mores the pity. Now let's find this friend of yours, do your business, and we can be on our way."

"This might take some time. You will have to wait for me."

Giacomo pulls a face.

"Hmm, I might just have to find some diversion to keep me busy. Do not try to leave without me, Dante, because I will not be leaving without you."

They put the stilts and cloak behind a heavy curtain and move along the hall towards the sound of music and loud voices. Rounding the corner they enter a large ballroom with several hundred costumed and masked guests.

At the far end of the room is a raised platform where musicians, mainly violinists, are playing. Dante works his way around the edge of the crowd who move out of his way as his wet disheveled appearance is not quite what they expect to see at a gathering such as this.

Giacomo, who is close behind him, is instantly recognised and is greeted with enthusiasm by those familiar with his so-called entertaining abilities. Dante finally arrives at the small stage and sees Luisa. She is concentrating on playing and fails to see him until he moves in front of her. She motions to the empty chair beside her where there is a violin case.

Mounting the stage Dante weaves his way through the musicians and taking up the case sits beside her. Without showing any surprise at his appearance, Luisa continues playing as she speaks to him.

"Good. You got my message."

Dante shakes his head.

"Message? No. What message?"

An exasperated Luisa replies.

"To be here, for this. I sent a message to your lodgings." She impatiently taps the sheet music on the stand in front of him.

"This is Carnevale season."

She begins playing again.

"Lots of occasions like this one. I thought you might need the money, so now earn it."

Suddenly she sees the blood on the back of his hand. She puts down her violin and takes a silk handkerchief from her waist band which she gently wraps around the wound.

"How did this happen?" she whispers.

Dante smiles.

"A large gang of cutthroats tried to stop me coming here to see you. I had to fight them off."

She pushes his hand away and picks up her violin.

"Liar! Now play!"

Still smiling Dante puts the violin to his shoulder and frantically scans the sheet music in front of him. Luisa taps the sheet music with her bow.

"If you can't follow then mime."

He does exactly that until the sheets are turned and then he joins in.

"Incidentally, I didn't get any message. I've been out all day. And thank you. I do need the money."

He turns to look at her.

"I felt the need to see you again. I've been looking everywhere for you."

"Really? So now you have found me, you can calm down and stop fighting in the alleys."

She smiles at him.

"In spite of your injuries, you are actually playing very well."

"If you left a message with Antonio, I haven't seen him in almost two days."

Still playing she answers him.

"I did. He has been busy on something; probably forgotten to tell you anyway."

"When did you see him?"

"He called round. He owed me some money."

Dante suddenly stops playing and removes the violin from his shoulder and looks at it.

"This is mine."

"Of course it is. I had Antonio bring it here in case you turned up, which you have."

She taps him on the knee with the bow.

"Now concentrate, finish this piece and we can talk."

Dante grins. He is now sitting beside a girl he has slowly become besotted with and playing beautiful music on his own violin. He strikes the strings of his instrument with the bow in a sign of exuberance. Luisa frowns at him and shakes her head in mock anger.

Giacomo Grande has seen all of this from the side of the stage. His usually happy smiling face is now wearing a frown

Chapter 31

The rear doors from the main salon swing open on to a corridor and Luisa hurries through, pulling Dante behind her. She has an opened bottle of wine in her hand and Dante is carrying both of their violins.

Raising the bottle she takes a long gulp and then hands it to Dante. She laughs as Dante takes a long drink.

"Straight from the bottle, no glasses. It works quicker that way."

Handing the bottle back, Dante nods in the direction of the ballroom.

"We have to stop coming to these classy events."

Luisa leans against the wall.

"There is no-one in there with any class, especially that odious little dwarf. He keeps leering at you."

"His name is Giacomo, Giacomo Grande."

Luisa is slightly shocked.

"You know him?"

Slightly surprised at her reaction he laughs.

"Worse than that. He is coming back to my lodgings when we finish here."

An open mouthed Luisa stares at him as he continues.

"There is something there that belongs to him and he desperately wants it back."

She takes another long drink from the bottle.

"What?"

Dante now has a slight attack of the giggles and she prods at him to answer.

"What is it?"

"His codpiece; we stole it from him."

"We?"

"It's a long story, and complicated, but I promised that I would give it back to him tonight."

She pulls him close to her by his shirt front and looks into his eyes.

"This is a story I must hear. When you have given your little friend his codpiece back then you must come and tell me all about it."

They hold the look for a long moment then she gently pushes him away.

"Now back to the fray."

She takes another drink, hands him the almost empty bottle, and with a quick smile slips through the doors into the main salon. Dante is in a daze; all of his wildest dreams are just falling into place. Throwing the bottle to the floor, he follows her.

Chapter 32

Two small oil lamps and a variety of run down candles illuminate the tiny attic room.

Clothes are being thrown into the air from the back of a narrow straw mattress cot.

Giacomo sits on the only chair, patiently watching proceedings as a sweaty Dante appears from the end of the bed.

"I'm sure it's here."

He looks at Giacomo.

"We have never used it, I promise."

Giacomo merely murmurs.

"I would be able to tell."

Dante nods and disappears again to search among the clothes. As he does so, two small green bottles roll out across the floor. Dante has not noticed them but Giacomo does and he picks one up, unplugs the cork stopper, sniffs at the neck of the bottle, replaces the stopper and slides the bottle into his waistcoat pocket.

Still under the cot and searching frantically, Dante asks, "What's so precious about it anyway? You could always buy another one, an unused one."

Giacomo smiles to himself.

"Apart from your friend who stole it from me, no-one else was allowed to touch it. Just me."

Dante re-appears above the cot. Rests his chin on the mattress and slowly raises his right hand.

"Got it!"

The shabby looking codpiece hangs from his hand. Without saying a word Giacomo leaps from his chair, bounds across the bed and snatches it. A startled Dante watches as an obviously delighted Giacomo dances around the room holding the codpiece in front of him. He is grinning from ear to ear.

"Why is it so important to you?"

Giacomo does not answer but pulls a sharp stiletto from his tunic and begins to use the point of it to unpick the stitching at the base of the codpiece. As he does the cojones part starts to come away from the body of the fake penis. When the sac is completely free Giacomo leaps off the cot and begins to dance around the room once more. He sings a little song to himself as he waves the silken testicle sac above his head.

Dante watches in amazement.

"You wanted the cojones?"

Giacomo is now beside himself with glee and he laughs out loud.

"Special cojones."

And he dances over to Dante, holding out the small silk bag.

"Now my young friend, squeeze my balls."

Dante pulls a face and shakes his head.

"No thanks."

This causes Giacomo to laugh out loud again and he does another little dance around the room before returning to Dante.

"Would I be correct in thinking you have only ever felt your own?"

Dante nods vigorously. Giacomo looks slyly at him.

"I thought so, foolish boy."

He thrusts the silken bag in front of Dante's face.

"But I insist you feel mine."

Dante once again shakes his head. Giacomo waves a finger at him.

"No? You will never ever feel cojones like Giacomo Grande's."

The small man sits on the cot and squeezes the silken bag. It makes a scrunching sound.

"What's in there? What's making that noise?"

Giacomo puts the bag near Dante's ear and squeezes it again.

"That my friend is the sound of freedom, my freedom."

As he says this he crunches the small silken sack again. This time it suddenly splits open and he desperately tries to stop the contents from falling out. Dante cannot believe his eyes as a dozen or so large diamonds fall onto the mattress. The stones catch the light from the candles in the room and sparkle.

He looks at Giacomo.

"Diamonds? How did you get these? They must be worth a fortune."

Giacomo frantically scoops up the gems.

"Indeed, they are worth a fortune."

He holds them up to his face as he looks at Dante.

"I worked all my life for these stones, Dante."

Dante catches on to Giacomo's sudden sombre mood as he continues.

"When fate throws you out into the world looking like me, there are very few choices in life."

He smiles to himself.

"How do I survive? By being a joke, a figure of fun and derision; by becoming a joker, then an entertainer."

He slaps his backside.

"By being the butt of all jokes."

Dante nods and then speaks quietly, trying not to break the mood.

"You must have been very well paid, Giacomo."

Holding up all of the jewels in the palm of his hand, Giacomo shows them to Dante and laughs as he replies.

"They were all stolen, over many years."

"So you are a thief?"

Dante is genuinely shocked.

"No, not a thief. These are payment for my degradation."

"What degradation?"

Giacomo takes a moment to answer.

"Years of the insults, the humiliation, abuse, sexual depravity, and worst of all….."

He looks up at Dante and gives a little laugh.

"……her bad breath."

Dante recoils a little.

"The Countess?"

"Who else?"

Giacomo seems to withdraw into some other place as he continues.

"She wanted a pet, an obedient animal, a human one. That unfortunate honour fell on me."

He keeps staring at the diamonds in his hand as the memories seem to come back to him.

"She bought me from my parents, my loving parents. I suppose they had no choice really, but may they rot in hell."

He gives another humourless little laugh, squeezes the diamonds together, and it is a moment or two before he speaks again.

"She uses me as a toy, anything she requests, orders, commands, I do."

He casts a quick glance at Dante, who is totally mesmerized by his story, and shakes his head as if trying to get rid of some picture in his brain.

"Every time she asked me to do certain things, I made her pay; I stole one of her precious diamonds."

Again he looks at Dante.

"If you think she has bad breath, then that is just the beginning."

Dante grimaces slightly. He manages a little sympathetic smile which helps change Giacomo's mood. Brightening up a little, he adds.

"Anyway she has so many diamonds she will never miss these and they will buy me my freedom and some comfort in my old age. I do not entertain as much as I once did."

He casts a glance at Dante.

"A simple plan, yes?"

"Very simple; almost faultless, except if she realises. She will know it is you. They still hang thieves, I believe."

Giacomo rocks back and forth slightly.

"There was a time I almost told her. Hanging seemed a brighter prospect than dealing with her daily demands. But my natural zest for living kept me going."

He reaches out and touches Dante gently on the arm.

"When your friend stole them from me, my world almost ended. Then the Countess mentioned he was with Mozart's orchestra, so I came here to find him."

"And found me instead."

"And that worked to our mutual advantage. You kept your life and I got back my stones."

As he speaks he places the stones on the bedcover and rubs his hand over them. Dante gets off the floor and sits opposite him.

Giacomo picks up each stone and looks at it against the candle light. After checking all of them, he picks one out and hands it to Dante.

"This small one is yours."

Dante pushes his hand away and shakes his head.

"No thanks. I don't want it: It's stolen property."

Giacomo has a puzzled grin on his face.

"Only you and I know that. Take it."

He pushes the stone back to Dante.

"Giacomo, I don't need it."

Giacomo bursts out laughing.

"Need, what is need?"

He looks around the squalid little room.

"Oh, I see! This is the Doge's Palace! Silly me, I thought you were a penniless musician. Please forgive me!"

"Alright, so you don't need it. What do you want then?"

"Nothing." Dante hesitates. "And everything."

Giacomo stares at him.

"The girl, the fiddler? You want her?"

Dante takes some moments to answer and he does this by slowly nodding.

Giacomo is still holding out the sparkling stone.

"Then you will definitely need this, to give you what you seem to want."

Dante slowly holds out his hand and Giacomo places the stone in his palm and folds his fingers over it.

Still holding his hand Giacomo pulls Dante even closer.

"One thing I learned at the knee of the Countess, and quite often between her scrawny, stringy thighs, is that it is the prerogative of the corrupt to corrupt others; it is also one of life's darker pleasures."

Suddenly, he leaps up onto the bed and roaring with laughter he gives a little jig.

"You are now a thief, just like me. No-one but you knows about these stones, Dante. By taking one you are as guilty as I am. If you tell anyone about them then we will surely share a jig on the gallows. That is not a gift; it is to buy your silence."

He grins at Dante.

"The other way to keep you silent is somewhat messy."

He releases Dante's hand, carefully scoops up the rest of the diamonds and dashes to the door. As he opens it he turns.

"Enjoy it boy. It will either buy the bedrock for your future prosperity and happiness or the first seeds of your depravity."

He leaves the room and slams the door shut. Dante sits on the bed and listens to him noisily dancing down the stairs.

He looks at the diamond in the palm of his hand, shrugs his shoulders and then gently pushes it under the blood stained silk wrap covering his wound.

Chapter 33

Dante climbs the last few stairs to Luisa's lodgings. When he arrives he listens at the door for a few moments, then wipes his brow with a neckerchief, runs his fingers through his hair, damping down the more rebellious locks and gently knocks on the old beam door.

He waits, listens, and is about to knock once again when the door suddenly swings open.

Luisa is standing there smiling at him. He can see she has taken some care with her appearance. She is beautiful.

Behind her the room is softly lit by a multitude of candles and the light casts subtle shades and highlights on her long hair.

Dante is speechless, completely in awe of her beauty, so he just smiles at her.

Luisa reaches forward and slowly pulls him into her room, quietly closing the door behind him.

The room is comfortably furnished with a couch, two chairs at a small table, and a large bed. A fire is burning. She leads Dante across to the fireplace and faces him.

"Did you find what the dwarf was after?"

"Yes."

She smiles.

"His beloved codpiece. He must have been glad to have it back."

Dante strokes his chin.

"Very glad. It meant an awful lot to him. Apparently it was a gift from his Patron, a Countess. It brought back many memories for him. He said it was a valuable keepsake."

They stand there for a few moments, just looking into each other's eyes.

"Are you hungry, Dante?"

"Yes, yes I am."

She moves slightly closer to him.

"How hungry?"

Slightly bemused, Dante looks around. There is no food in sight.

"Very."

Without another word, Luisa reaches up with both hands and hooks her thumbs below the top of her dress. In a moment she has slipped it off her shoulders and it drops to the floor. She stands naked before him.

"Good. So am I. You are the first course; I am the second."

She kneels down in front of him and deftly undoes his breeches. With a sharp tug she pulls them down and buries her face into his crotch, nuzzling his rapidly growing penis.

A stunned Dante watches as she places his penis into her mouth and begins to move on him. It takes only a few moments before he places his hands on each side of her head and pulls her off his now fully erect cock.

Luisa stands, kisses him, then whispers in his ear, "Fuck me, Dante. Just simply fuck me."

Chapter 34

The weak dawn sun is desperately trying to break through the thick layer of rain cloud and Franco Gabriele with his son Bruno are attempting to hitch a bullock to a small plough.

The cold wind whips at their heavy clothes and they both pull their knitted woollen hats further down on their heads. Even the bullock is feeling the cold and tries to turn its rear into the wind.

This is not the direction Franco wants him to go and so begins a small tussle between two tons of animal and a small but determined human. Franco resorts to hitting it with a stick when a faint voice drifts across the rocky field. Father Emanuele is at the bottom of the field and he is waving a piece of paper.

"Franco!"

His shouts are being fragmented by the wind and he starts to climb up the field to get nearer. Franco takes the opportunity to rest from his battle with his bovine opponent and father and son lean against it to collect some of the animals warmth as they watch the priest stumble up the slight incline towards them.

A slightly breathless but also elated priest finally arrives and he too takes advantage of the bulk of the bullock. All three of them crouch down behind it as Franco waits for his brother to get his breath back.

"It is a little early in the day for me to be hiking these hills, Franco."

The farmer laughs.

"This is not a hill, brother."

He looks around.

"Hardly a hillock! You should do more exercise. Saying mass will not make you powerful, not in this world at least. What brings you out here anyway?"

Still slightly breathless, Emanuele waves the paper in front of Franco's face.

"This. A letter!"

Franco shrugs.

"Who is it from?"

Shaking his head, Emanuele laughs.

"Who do you think? Your other son. Dante. Remember him?"

This brings a sharp response from Franco.

"Of course I do. What does he say?"

"Here, read it."

The priest holds out the letter which is pushed straight back at him.

"You know I cannot read well. You were the clever one at school."

"I know and I can teach you any time."

"Of course, all we need is another day in every week. Read it!"

Fishing out a pair of thick spectacles and leisurely placing them on his nose, he is hurried along by the bullock becoming impatient and making a move for the shelter of the sparse hedgerow. Franco hits it sharply with his stick which changes the animals mind.

"Come on man, read it! Even the beast is impatient."

Leaning in towards his brother in order to try and stop the paper fluttering, Emanuele reads Dante's short letter. When he is finished he folds it neatly and puts it into a pocket in Franco's care worn jacket.

"Anna might want to keep it, as a memento."

The wind has seemingly brought a slight tear to Franco's eye and he turns away to wipe it.

"It might be the only thing she gets to keep. He seems to be making a living then, doing what he wants to do."

Emanuele nods.

"Aye, it is a successful and satisfying life if we can all get to do that."

A moment's silence descends over them and then Franco begins to resume fixing the harness on the bullock.

"Right, got a field to plough."

He looks at the priest.

"It's exactly what I want to do, and you can go and save some souls. We should all have a satisfying day."

Emanuele smiles at his younger brother and places a hand on his shoulder as he turns to go.

"Yes, we should, and I hope that Dante is having one too."

The two men go about their tasks as the priest walks carefully down the hill, pulling a slight face as he hears his brother gives the bullock another whack with his stick.

Chapter 35

Dante is sleeping soundly when Luisa's hand slowly slips under the thin cotton sheet that covers him. It emerges again holding his hand. Carefully she kisses the small scar on the back.

He opens his eyes to see her smiling face just a few inches away from his.

"Wake up."

She swiftly pulls the sheet to one side and gets into bed beside him, nuzzling her face into his neck.

"It's a beautiful sunrise. The mornings are the best. I can see you!"

She raises the sheet and peers down the bed.

"All of you! And now I want my breakfast."

Without another word she slides down the bed.

Dante, now wide awake makes a feeble attempt to stop her but he is laughing as much as she is and lies back, pulling the sheet over his head.

They laugh and gasp almost at the same time as some sensitive part of one of their bodies is touched, stroked, pulled or bitten. The sheet covers both of them and looks like some enormous wriggling creature. It doesn't resemble anything human until at last they stop and lay side by side under the thin cotton cover.

After a few moment's rest, Luisa's hand reaches out under the bed where it finds her violin and bow. Still shrouded in the cover, she sits up and puts her leg over Dante. Keeping the cover over her she begins to play the instrument.

Luisa slowly moves her body in time with the music. The tune is a gypsy one and involves lots of deep sweeping moves. She follows this with her body, still sitting astride her lover. She grinds herself into Dante's groin as the music picks up pace and her hips begin to move rapidly. As the music becomes faster, she misses a number of notes which makes Dante laugh out loud. But then she finds the rhythm again and continues to grind into him.

They are both now moving in sexual synchronisation. Luisa leans in towards him as the music and the pair of them start to reach the finale.

The climax arrives for all three at same time. Luisa throws off the sheet as Dante bucks up against her. Both of them gasp with the intense pleasure that only an orgasm can achieve.

The end of the bow is sticking into his chest but Luisa is oblivious to all except the waves of that sweet orgasmic pain that make her sit upright and press down on him wanting more.

The violin slips from her grasp and she clutches the mattress. The moment seems to last forever for both of them and then when it starts to subside she slowly drops down onto Dante's sweating body and pushes her face into his neck again.

After a minute or so she rolls off and lies beside him giving a little laugh.

"Now that is what I call music. We must never come to bed without the violin."

Dante says nothing. There is no need. The contented smile on his face says it all.

Chapter 36

The three mast galleon is moored to one of the quieter wharfs at the northern end of the Grand Canal. The wharf is faced by tall warehouses, small taverns, some little inns and one or two brazenly advertised brothels. Some early morning drifters wander past the closed taverns waiting for them to open. The area is quiet at this early hour but in a short time it will be teeming with wharf workers and horse drawn coaches.

The large vessel is tied securely to the thick steel hoops that are anchored in massive square blocks of Dolomite granite. The noise from the ship's rigging is constant even though there is virtually no wind, just a slight breeze from the Adriatic Sea drifting over the lagoon and its reed marshes.

The door to the Captain's quarters swings open and two men emerge onto the deserted deck. They quickly cross to the gangplank where they shake hands and one of them walks as steadily as he can down the slightly swaying ladder.

The man on the deck watches until the other one reaches the wharf and then with a brief wave he makes his way back through the doorway.

The man on the wharf quickly strides along until he finds an alleyway which he enters. The small sea breeze is slightly stronger in the confined space and it whips up the man's cloak to reveal a violin case slung over his shoulder. It also dislodges the thick scarf which hides his face.

Stopping briefly, the man adjusts both his cloak and the scarf, pulls down his hat and continues on his way.

Chapter 37

Dante's sweating face pushes up from beneath the almost sodden sheets. He wipes the perspiration from his forehead.

"God, that was close."

He lifts the sheet and peers down the bed.

"We have to make this last."

Luisa wraps her arms around his neck and she pulls him back under the covers.

"There's lots more, Dante. Eat from the feast."

The two of them once again seem to merge into one frantic animal as they move into each other. It takes only a few moments before they both climax once again. A stillness settles over the bed.

"If only we could make music as well as we make love, Dante."

Dante says nothing in reply as he makes his way up the bed, kissing and nuzzling her body as he goes. Eventually he appears at the top and lies on top of her, gazing into her face.

Stroking her sweat sodden hair he whispers, "You are so beautiful. Promise you will never change."

Luisa whispers back to him, "I need you here, all the time."

Rolling to one side, Dante stares at the ceiling as he contemplates what Luisa has just said. She pokes him gently with a finger.

"Would that be a concern for you, Dante?"

A smile creeps across his face as he turns to her.

"I never, ever want to be away from you for the rest of my life."

She snuggles closer, kisses him on the cheek.

"Does that mean a 'Yes' then?"

There is no reply as Dante rolls over and kisses her.

Chapter 38

Some months later

Dante is practicing some chords on his violin when Luisa bursts in. Her cheeks are flushed and she is very excited; she is holding a folded piece of paper.

Dashing across to Dante who is sitting on the bed, she throws her arms around his neck and kisses him.

"He has done it."

Quietly laughing, Dante gently pushes her away so that he can see her face.

"Who has done what?"

"Antonio. He has got you a job."

She waves the paper in front of his face.

"I met Lorenzo outside. He was about to deliver this note. Antonio has had to go to another concert and he has passed this one on to you."

Dante takes the note from her and reads it.

"It is on a mountain above Belluno, wherever that is. An establishment for young ladies who are dedicating their lives to the works of the Christian faith."

He looks at her.

"Nuns?"

She laughs as she gets up from him.

"No, not necessarily; just ardent worshippers."

He looks at the note again.

"There are no details here."

She holds up another note.

"I have them. You are to travel tomorrow. It is almost two days by coach. You are to stay for one week. They are particularly eager to learn some religious pieces, that's why he probably thought it would suit you."

Dante lies back on the bed.

"Wonderful! Two days by coach. How do you suppose I pay for that?"

She reads from the note again.

"Easy. You don't have to. You are reserved on the coach that leaves in the morning from the coach inn. You have a seat paid for."

Dante sits up.

"This is my first engagement as a lone artist!"

He preens a little.

"I am a professional musician at last!"

A laughing Luisa sits on his lap.

"You have to go and do it first Mr. Musician. Two days on a coach and then a week with devout religious women. Hard work."

Dante pinches her on the nose.

"You are right. I have never really met any devout women before. They must be hard work."

She laughs as she sits astride him.

"Not as hard as me."

They wrap themselves around each other and fall back onto the bed kissing frantically as they rip each other's clothes off.

Chapter 39

The bedroom of the Countess Margarethe of Waldstadten is a sumptuous affair lit by many candelabra. The walls are covered in lavishly painted country scenes featuring deer, mountains, lakes, forests and an occasional glimpse of lovers hidden by discreetly placed shrubs. The paintings are framed by thick velvet curtains.

Around the room are lots of chairs and small tables with flagons of wine and trays of sweetmeats. The Countess enjoys having company when she takes to her bed and she treats her carefully selected guests generously. The bed itself is as ornate as any that has ever been devised during this period of total extravagance and the Countess is sitting in the middle of the wide mattress playing a violin. Her audience of friends listen attentively as she performs on the instrument and they all applaud vigorously when she finishes the short piece. Then they rapidly resume quaffing the fine wine and filling their faces with the very best that a well equipped kitchen and a team of talented cooks can provide.

There is a buzz of excitement in the large room as the Countess prepares herself for more entertainment. Tonight is a special night, one of many that she has arranged over the last year or so; tonight word has spread that she has a special tutor who is going to teach her some extraordinary techniques.

The Countess is assisted by two maids who move her down the bed and stack piles of silken pillows behind her; another of her maids busily undoes the outer clothing and strips away layer after layer of fine underwear.

Eventually the Countess is sitting propped up in her bed wearing only the most sheer of silken shifts. The thin material is totally ineffective in covering up the shape of the woman, and her nipples and thick bush of pubic hair are clearly visible. Modesty is not the first thing on the mind of the Countess and she hungrily watches as her tutor enters the room.

The man is tall and muscular, wearing only a loin cloth and a full face mask. He walks proudly from an anteroom and moves to the bed. The audience are more than interested and murmur appreciatively as he settles on the bed. He carries two violin cases. He carefully puts one on the end of the bed behind him. The other one he opens and takes out a violin and bow. Turning to the other case he opens it and reveals a silk scarf. A man in the audience leans over, puts his hand under the scarf, removes a small green bottle and leaves a gold coin in its place. Other guests begin to do the same as the tutor places some pillows behind himself.

When the tutor is in position he slowly removes his loin cloth. He is naked and the proud possessor of an erect penis.

The mood in the room begins to change and the guests start to edge closer to the bed. Some of the women avert their eyes, but only for a moment.

The tutor beckons to the Countess's maids and they move to the bed. Two of them on each side of the old woman move her down the bed. She opens her legs and pulls up the silken shift to reveal her thick pubic bush.

The tutor is now sitting with his legs splayed and the maids gently lift their mistress onto his very rigid penis. As they lower her, another gives her a violin and with a tremble she puts it to her chin. The Countess settles comfortably on the many pillows and gives a little sigh of contentment as she wriggles on her new perch.

The tutor remains impassive as this happens. The only sign of any discomfort in his composure is a trickle of sweat which runs down onto his chin from under the mask and drips onto his bare chest. The Countess leans forward to touch it but the tutor gently pushes her hand away and taps her violin with his bow.

The Countess's very thin, almost fleshless thighs are spread over the tutor's well-muscled legs and she leans back slightly as she begins to play.

The music is slow at first and then it moves into a faster tempo. The Countess is barely paying any attention as she moves her thin buttocks as hard as she can against her musical partner.

The audience, whilst almost completely silent, begin to have their own sexual activity and the small bottles are rapidly passed around as skirts are lifted and some less than elegant seating arrangements take place.

The tutor is now playing some very fast music and seems to have moved into a world of his own, oblivious to the audience around him. As he does so, he moves his head rapidly, so much so that his long blonde ponytail tied up with a ribbon, falls down onto his shoulders. No-one seems to notice or care.

Chapter 40

It is still dark and very chilly as Dante, still half asleep, steps out onto the landing and folds his arms around an equally sleepy Luisa.

"I still cannot believe that I am leaving you, even for a few days. You are so much a part of my life, my entire being; I feel as though I am being torn apart."

He nuzzles into her neck and smells her hair.

"These past few months have given me my life, my reason for being. I love you Luisa and always will."

A very sleepy Luisa nods and moves to kiss him.

"If you do not go and earn some money, my love, then you will be coming back to a skeleton."

She pushes him gently away from her.

"We seem to have been living on love, but we must surely run out of that shortly; now go and earn your keep, Mr. Musician."

Dante reluctantly lets her go and almost stumbles down the stairs. He stops on his way down and looks back to see Luisa standing in the doorway. He blows her a kiss and she responds by slowly opening her dressing gown to display her naked body. Dante begins to move back up the stairs but she puts out her hand to stop him and motions for him to go.

With last lingering looks, the lovers part company and Dante moves out into the cold dawn light.

The coach inn is at the end of the road that leads to the mainland and a small crowd has gathered around the several large horse drawn coaches.

A little display board indicates where each of the coaches will be and what their ultimate destination is. Dante finds his allotted coach at the far end and when he gets to it he peers inside the small window. The inside is packed with several people sitting on the laps of other passengers.

The shaven headed driver is busy tying bags of luggage onto the roof of the vehicle and barely looks at Dante when he asks where his seat is.

"Seat? You want a seat, you get here at midnight."

Dante waves his travel docket supplied by Antonio.

"It says here, one seat inside the coach."

The driver carries on without looking at Dante.

"You want a seat, you'd better tell them. They all paid for seats, too."

He motions to the passengers already crammed inside the coach.

"This is theft."

Stacking up another pile of bags, the driver turns and grins at Dante.

"Yeh! Clever lad, ain't ya?"

"I demand to see whoever is in charge. I want a refund."

The driver sits down on a large bag and rubs a hand over his stubbly head.

"The man in charge, eh? That would be me."

Dante waves his ticket at him.

"Then you are a thief."

The man nods and grins.

"Probably."

A furious Dante begins to get exasperated.

"What are you going to do about it?"

The driver stands up and seems to consider Dante's question as he ties down the baggage.

"Nothing. What are you going to do about it?"

"I will report you to the authorities."

The man nods and points to a building across the road.

"You need to go in there. Opens in about four hours."

"Right. I will get some sense and some money refunded."

The driver climbs off the roof of the coach and settles in his seat.

"Right."

He takes the whip out of its holder and has a sample snap just above the ears of the two front horses. They immediately begin to pull against the shafts of the heavy laden vehicle. Dante walks to the front and looks up at the driver.

"What are you doing?"

"What I do. I drive. Get out of the way, or get trampled."

Dante leaps to one side as the driver snaps his long whip again. Now all four horses begin to slowly pull the coach into motion. He walks alongside.

"How will I get to my destination?"

The driver looks down at him as he gathers speed. The metal clad wheels clanking over the cobbled roadway.

"You have two choices. You either follow this coach on foot or you can travel up here on top."

He pats a large leather bag and grins.

"Very comfortable."

Dante is now furious.

"I will get my seat or my money back. Stop this coach right now."

The driver spits into the road and sends the long leather thong snaking above the ears of the lead horse. He laughs as he passes a distraught Dante who can only watch him make his way to the mainland causeway.

Chapter 41

The knocking on the door is gentle at first and then after several attempts it gets louder.

Luisa is in a very heavy sleep and has accommodated the knocking into a dream. The knocking persists and with a start she suddenly wakes up.

"Yes? Who is it?"

There is a muffled reply.

"Bazzo?"

"Yes. Who are you?"

"Package for a Bazzo."

Luisa begins to get out of bed, falls back and tries again. She reaches for a dressing gown which she just throws over her shoulders and walks slowly, almost painfully to the door, opening it just slightly. Through the crack she sees a boy of thirteen or so, a street urchin, looking up at her.

"You Bazzo?"

She nods and the boy suddenly thrusts a small, paper wrapped parcel at her. She grabs it as he hurtles off down the stairs.

Climbing back into the bed she turns the small package over in her hands and then slowly begins to undo the string that is tied around it.

Chapter 42

The road leading down into the town of Lago Santa Croce is steep and the driver keeps applying his brake lever. Occasionally the jerking movement wakes Dante who is huddled up behind him.

The wind from the high Dolomites is chilly; the lake is choppy and the small fishing boats moored off shore are bobbing furiously as they are tossed about. The town is in darkness; only a few shutters are open in its narrow streets and are banging noisily in the wind. The coach clatters along the stony roadway until it enters a wider space that rejoices in the name of Piazza Santa Croce.

The Piazza faces the lake and is deserted. A sign saying 'Locanda' hangs from a large house with a glass front door revealing the warmth of a low light from within. The driver aims for the 'Locanda' and pulls the brake.

Dante peers out from under the canvas cover that he pulled over his head when they entered the mountain region many hours previously, and looks around the square.

"Is this where we stay?"

The driver laughs as he begins to climb down off his seat.

"No. The coach leaves again in four hours."

"Four hours? Are you going to drive all through the night?"

Knocking on the doors of the coach, the driver looks up at him.

"Not me. This is where I go to the bosom of my favourite harlot and where I will stay for at least twelve hours. You have another driver for the onward journey."

Dante begins to stretch his cramped and aching limbs.

"How much further to my destination?"

The driver is already making his way into the Locanda after tying up the horses.

"Where are you going?"

Peering at his ticket in the gloom, Dante makes out the words.

"Monte Toc."

Blowing on his hands before he enters the hostelry, which is becoming more welcoming by the moment, he answers.

"Monte Toc. That's hours away. What are you going there for?"

"To teach some music."

"There's nothing there. Just a mountain and the monastery, and that closed down years ago."

"Nuns. I am going to teach some nuns."

The driver gives a little derisory snort as he pushes open the door and disappears inside. Then he shouts back over his shoulder.

"Nuns. Them women are not nuns."

Dante nods in agreement but the man is now inside so he finishes the sentence almost to himself.

"No, they are training to become nuns."

His comment did not fall on deaf ears as some of the passengers from the coach hurry past him to the warmth of the Locanda. One or two cast looks in Dante's direction as they go by.

Slowly climbing down from the coach to the road, Dante pulls a small purse from his pocket. There are only a few coins inside and he moves across to where a list of food that is available is scrawled on a board outside the entrance. A quick count and a re-check of the prices and Dante pushes his way inside.

Chapter 43

The grey dawn light slants across the ploughed field as Franco swings a large axe into a solid piece of timber. The axe make only a slight impression in the thick bark and Franco pulls it out and picks up a long broad toothed saw.

The low wagon behind him is already piled high with sawn wood from the old oak tree that had fallen over the previous evening in a high wind.

He watches as Emanuele struggles to throw a large log onto the pile and then takes the handle on the other end of the saw from his brother.

"Enough to keep us warm for a whole winter here."

"Yes, and the church."

This remark is ignored by Franco as the two men set about sawing through the thick branch. After a minute or so they stop to get their breath back. Emanuele sits on the branch and looks along the hedgerow.

"It's left a gap. Must have been here over a hundred years or so."

Franco nods.

"At one time there were two of them. They marked the boundaries of the land. When grandfather got married to grandmother from the farm next door, he chopped one down."

Emanuele looks at him.

"Really? I never heard that story before."

"Papa told me one day, just after you left to go priesting."

He smiles at his elder brother, knowing the word would get a slight reaction.

"He thought it was symbolic, a joining of two people, two small farms, making it into one family. No barriers."

They sit for a moment or two and then Franco resumes his tale.

"Grandfather used the timber for all of the house furniture, everything: tables, chairs, beds, and then cots for the children, and toys."

The thought brings a smile to both of them.

"He even kept some stored away in the barn and then made their coffins from it."

"The tree served them well then?"

"Aye. Nothing like an oak coffin to lie in. Keeps the worms away for some time!"

Emanuele points to the hedgerow.

"What are you going to put into the gap?"

"Olives. I can get a couple of them in there. They will serve us well, too. But first we will have to move that root."

He points to the jagged edges of the trunk that are all that remain in the ground of the giant oak tree.

Emanuele laughs.

"Not today, brother. We have another week's work just sawing up the branches."

He pats the thick heavy bough.

"Keep a bit of this for me, Franco. I like the idea of being wrapped in a part of our history."

Franco stands up and takes hold of the saw again.

"It will have rotted by the time you need it. C'mon."

He smiles at his brother as he moves the saw along the branch.

"How tall are you, just in case?"

Chapter 44

The road north from Lago Santa Croce clings to the side of a steep hill as it skirts the river that feeds the lake. The green-blue coloured river water which is fresh from the snow melt bubbles over the white rocks about a hundred feet below the gravel pathway.

Dante moves closer to the centre of the coach top and subconsciously looks for a safe place to land if the vehicle should suddenly topple over. The new driver displays much more confidence and gently flicks his long whip to encourage the lead horses to put more effort into getting the heavy coach up the long incline.

Rounding a bend in the road, the true majesty of the high peaks becomes visible. Sharp snow-capped mountains tower over the valley and the road ahead as far as Dante can see runs along the bottom of the valley.

There is no sign of any habitation outside of the perimeter of the small lakeside town they had just left, and the silence of the mountains is broken only by the sound of the coach wheels and the creaking of the harnesses. Occasionally they pass a small brook which tumbles down a steep rock face and forces its way underground as it hits the roadway.

The beauty and solitude of the area makes a deep impression on Dante and he settles back to enjoy the ride as much as he can. This enjoyment is spoiled slightly by his rumbling stomach and his cold cramped seating arrangement. The Locanda where the coach had stopped last night offered only rudimentary cooking and it took all of Dante's money to buy a small plate of very tough meat and some sour vegetables in a thin sauce.

The meat was almost inedible, so he finished up with just a few forkfuls of badly cooked potatoes and chewy carrots. He began to visualize the meal he would have when he arrived at his destination.

He leans forward to speak to the driver who had not uttered one word to him since he had taken over for this leg of the journey.

"How far to Monte Toc?"

The driver appears not to have heard him and he flicks at the horses' ears. Dante is about to ask again when he gets an answer.

"Time or distance?"

The man has not turned his head to answer so Dante shrugs his shoulders.

"Both I suppose."

Another pause from the driver as he considers his answer. Then he points to a very high mountain directly ahead of them, some miles away at the end of the valley.

"See that peak?"

Dante nods. It would be difficult not to see it as it lay straight ahead.

"Yes."

"Well your Monte Toc is directly behind that one."

Dante's heart sinks. It is obviously miles away and several hours.

The driver speaks again. "A bleak place is Monte Toc. Always pleased to get past it."

"Why?"

Once again the driver takes his time answering.

"Not a good place. Even the monks had to leave after two hundred years. Now it's rumoured that some religious females have moved into the old monastery. Must be desperate to get away from the rest of the world. It could be asked why."

For the first time he looks at Dante, his face a complete blank.

"It could be asked why a young man like yourself would want to go there."

Dante is slightly flustered at the man's statement.

"To teach music. Only for a week."

After flicking at the horses again, the driver suddenly begins to pull a large waxed cotton rain cover from under his seat and spreads it across his shoulders and across the top of the seat. He also puts a large wide brimmed hat on his head and continues the conversation.

"Four hours, at the quickest. Unless that bursts on us, then it'll be a wet six."

He casually points up to the sky.

Looking directly up into what a few moments ago was a deep blue cloudless sky, Dante is astonished to see a massive thunderstorm gathering force over the high peak. Already flashes of lightning are visible.

The first large drops of rain begin to fall. Dante quickly moves across to the driver and pulls some of the waxed cover over his head, making sure his violin case and small bag are with him.

Chapter 45

Luisa is kneeling on the floor of her room. Between sobs of pain she vomits into a chamber pot. The sweat is rolling down her face and all the time she trembles.

Eventually the trembling stops and so does the vomiting. Completely exhausted she crawls over to the bed and pulls herself onto it, collapsing into the sweat soaked pillow.

After a short while she reaches under the pillow and takes out a small green bottle. Uncorking it, she takes a long swallow, then puts the bottle carefully down onto the floor.

Chapter 46

The driver was absolutely right in his estimate of the time it would take to reach the area of Monte Toc. He was also right in saying it would be a wet journey.

The storm that suddenly appeared above them had developed and stayed over the valley. The rain had never ceased and even with the protection of the waxed cover the damp had permeated through and Dante is now shivering with cold.

The foot of Monte Toc is covered in deep pine forest and as it is still raining heavily the trees have managed to trap a thick mist and visibility is down to about fifty yards.

Dante gets a surprise when the driver applies the brake handle and pulls at the reins to stop the coach.

"Here it is. Monte Toc."

Looking out from the cover of the tarpaulin Dante cannot see any sign that he has reached his destination.

"How do you know?"

"I know because I come here twice a week."

"But where is the monastery?"

The driver is in no mood for chatting and he keeps his answer brief, pointing into the thick mist.

"See that track?"

He indicates a narrow pathway through the trees.

"That takes you to the monastery. Just keep following it and you will get there."

"How far is it?"

"Depends on how fast you walk. The building is about three thousand feet up there."

Again he points upwards.

"You can't miss it. There is only one monastery on the mountain. If you walk past it then you will fall into the valley."

Dante hesitates for a moment.

"C'mon lad, get off! We have a long way to go."

Reluctantly Dante emerges from under his cover and the rain immediately begins to soak through his clothing.

Taking pity on him, the driver pulls another small square of waxed canvas from under his seat and hands it to him.

"I want it back when I pick you up here next week. Any time after 12 noon….."

Dante grabs the canvas and climbs down. The noise of the rain drowns out the next words from the driver.

"…..if you last that long."

Standing to one side of the narrow gravel roadway, Dante pulls the cover over his head and watches as the driver spurs his horses on and into the mist. His voice is slightly muffled as he shouts over his shoulder, "Don't be late; if you miss me then you walk."

Within moments the coach disappears and Dante takes stock of his situation.

Approaching the track the driver mentioned, he starts his trek. Almost immediately the trail begins to get steep and Dante begins to get out of breath. The only advantage of being among the trees is the rain is not quite as heavy; but, the path is muddy and very slippery underfoot which makes walking fast almost impossible.

As he walks he can hear the sound of thunder and it gets darker, not because of the time of day but because the clouds are beginning to get thicker. The effect is eerie and occasionally Dante carefully takes a nervous look over his shoulder. Wolves and bears are not uncommon in this part of the mountains. The only sounds he hears are his own breathing and footsteps, thunder and the constant patter of rain.

No matter how he holds the waxed cover, the constant rain manages to get through and Dante desperately tries to keep his bag and violin case covered. Realising that it is either him or his possessions that are inevitably going to get wet, he pulls the cover from over his head and wraps it tightly around the bag and case. Within a minute or so he is completely soaked to the skin.

He has now been climbing steadily uphill for over an hour; the light is fading fast and the rain is still relentless. In spite of himself, he is now nervous and slightly fearful. If darkness arrives before he gets to the monastery then he will have to stay the night in the woods. The thick mist which has been with him all the way up the track starts to thin out and Dante can see a little further through the dense forest.

Encroaching despair turns to elation when he suddenly sees a glimmer of light in the far distance across a deep valley. There on the other side of the ravine stands the monastery.

The grey stone building seems to have been converted from a castle or fort at one time. The castellated wall at one end faces out towards him and below it is a sheer drop down the rock face into the darkness.

To reach his destination Dante has to skirt the edge of the cliff which continues in a wide arc. At times the building seems quite close; then it disappears as the track meanders into the forest and returns to the cliff edge again.

It is during one of those occasions when he can no longer see the glow from one of the windows that he tops a little crest in the path and there before him, just several hundred yards away, is the rather forbidding front of the monastery.

Chapter 47

The single note from the metal doorbell echoes along the chiseled stone walled corridor. The low vaulted ceiling is lit by just a few candles in wall holders and the atmosphere is dark and gloomy. There is no sound or movement coming from the building.

Outside and huddled under the sparse overhang that protects the large double doors, Dante squeezes as near as he can under the shelter. He reaches up and is about to pull the bell rope a third time when the small iron grill in the centre of the door is slid to one side. Dante immediately pushes his face in front of it.

"My name is Gabriele, Dante Gabriele; music tutor."

Not a word is spoken by the person inside and the grille is snapped shut again. Dante steps back expecting the door to open but it doesn't.

He moves into the corner. His main aim is to protect his small bag and violin case which are still tightly wrapped in the waxed cover as the rain continues its steady downpour.

Several minutes pass before Dante hears the grille slide open again. A note is passed through. Dante grabs it and quickly reads.

Where is Signor Antonio?'

Dante pushes his face close to the grille.

"He cannot come. He has asked me to take his place. My name is Dante Gabriele, a friend of his."

He can see a dim shape, almost a silhouette, on the other side of the door. The figure is still and Dante feels he is being appraised. The grille slides shut and the large door begins to open.

The opening left for Dante to squeeze through is very narrow and he can barely make it. It takes a few moments for his eyes to adjust to the dim light and he eventually makes out a small figure dressed in what appears to be clerical clothing which lets him move past and then closes the door. Without saying a word the person moves along the corridor. Dante watches and then begins to follow.

As they pass one of the candles, Dante notes that the figure in front of him is in fact dressed as a nun. No wimple, just a tight headband. The uniform is slate grey and reaches to the floor which makes the nun seem to glide along the corridor. Not a word is spoken and he has to walk fast to keep up.

At the end of the corridor there is a short flight of stone steps which turn left into a shorter corridor. Again no furniture; no wall decorations. Not even a small painting or carved icon of any religious matter. Just bleak walls and except for the almost arrow slit windows there would be no light whatsoever in this part of the stark building.

The small nun stops abruptly and Dante almost collides with her as she turns a key in a thick wooden door. Stepping aside she motions for Dante to enter the room. A narrow cot and a chair are at one end; a spindle legged table with a candle stick and wash basin on it is the only other furnishing. The window is similar to the ones in the corridor outside: an arrow slit.

Dante takes a step into the room and looks around. As he does so, the door is quietly closed and he hears the key turn in the lock. He tries to turn the large iron door handle. It doesn't move. He bangs on the door. There is no sound from outside.

Walking to the bed he puts down his wrapped parcel and removes the violin case. On the small table there is a thin cotton towel that he uses to wipe down his case. On the bed, what first appears to be a bed cover is in fact a nun's dress, similar to the one his guide was wearing The dress is spread out as if waiting to be slipped into. At the neck Dante sees a corner of paper. He pulls it out and discovers it is another note.

'I am informed you are wet. Please take off your clothes and they will be collected and washed. We eat at seven o'clock. You will be escorted to the dining hall. Please avail yourself of the clothing we have left for you. I apologise for not having any male clothing available.'

The note is simply signed 'MS.'

Dante undoes his clothing. When he has stripped himself of everything, he wipes his still shivering body down with the damp towel. It is with a mixture of curiosity and some embarrassment that he pulls the nun's garment over his head, letting it fall to the ground. He is immediately comforted by the warmth that the woollen dress brings to him.

Quietly he tries the door again. It is still locked.

Sitting on the bed he opens the violin case and begins to tune the instrument.

There is no way of knowing the passage of time and he sits there watching the light fade from the room. He uses a flint lighter on the table to light the candle which he puts on the seat of the chair next to his bed. He pulls the thin blanket over himself and soon falls into a fitful sleep.

A light tap on the door slowly wakes him from a dream. It happens again, then the key is turned. At this point he is wide awake and sits up in the bed. His candle is now very low and through the slit window he can see total darkness outside.

Dante looks across to the doorway where a shadowy figure enters. The light from the lantern that the figure is carrying casts a large silhouette across the wall.

Dante's clothes are scooped up from where he had dropped them on the floor and the figure moves back out of the room. The door is left open and Dante throws the blanket to one side and jumps out of bed. Some sandals have been placed just under the bed and he slips them on. Walking across to the door he peers out.

The lantern carrying figure is now some yards away. It stops, turns and beckons. Dante needs no urging and he quickly moves along behind her. He is suddenly aware of just how hungry he is. The figure waits for him and when he catches up he sees it is a small woman whose face is almost completely in shadow. The woman points back to the door of his room.

He shakes his head.

"What is it you want?"

The woman points again, firmly.

It suddenly dawns on Dante that he is meant to either close the door or bring his violin. He swiftly does both and the pair of them resume their journey along the corridor. At the end they turn right and are immediately faced with some large steel studded doors. The guide bangs on them twice and within a moment or two they swing open.

The sight that greets Dante is so surprising that he has to blink his eyes a few times to get them used to the brightness, in stark contrast to the dark corridor and his room.

The dining hall, for that is where they are, is lit by dozens of thick candles, some in niches along the walls and some in wooden candle holders slung from the ceiling. There are two long tables that run the length of the room and about thirty nuns are sitting in complete silence. They all turn to watch him as he walks slowly forward.

"Signor Gabriele. Over here please."

Dante swings around to where the voice is coming from. To his right there is a raised platform which sits snugly into a wide niche in the wall. Also in this recess is a large log fire which is casting heat out even as far away as he is.

The caller is standing up and beckoning to him. The nun is tall, dressed in a black surplice and wearing a large white pointed wimple on her head.

As he makes his way towards her, he catches one or two glances from the nuns, some of whom cannot hide the smile on their faces. He suddenly realises why. The grey surplice he is wearing is slightly too short for him and his white legs and ankles are clearly visible. The dress is also wide in the skirt and it billows as he walks. He should be embarrassed but the smell of food and the heat from the fire are already overcoming the oddness of his situation.

The table is set for two. As he arrives, the nun takes his hand and shakes it. She indicates that he should sit on the chair next to her. They are now both facing the dining hall and all of the nuns. One quick look from his companion and the nuns turn their faces away and stare at the table.

The nun takes her time in addressing Dante. After staring at the assembled diners for a moment or two she turns to him.

"I am Sister Ita, the senior nun in this establishment; the Mother Superior."

"Ahh, MS."

She looks at him and he gets slightly flustered under her very icy gaze.

"The note you sent me, it was signed MS."

"Correct."

She abruptly turns away and clasps her hands on the table in front of her and bows her head. In a firm voice she a speaks to the assembly.

"Let us pray."

Dante copies her and bows his head. There is a murmur of prayer from the nuns but nothing from the woman beside him. He sneaks a little look and sees her lips moving but with no sound. She has her eyes tightly clenched and there is a slight smile on her face. When she stops she looks up. At that instant all of the nuns stop praying.

From the end of the room some other nuns begin to enter through a doorway which Dante surmises is the kitchen; two of them move to his table and begin to put out various dishes from large trays. The food is of a high quality with ham, chickens and vegetables, a tray of fresh baked bread.

The smell is overwhelming and without waiting Dante begins to fill his plate. The Mother Superior watches him for a moment and then does the same.

Completely forgetting his manners, Dante just starts to eat, his hunger overriding his sensitivities for a moment.

When he has a mouth full of food he glances at the Mother Superior. She has placed only two small portions of food on her plate and has not eaten any of it. She notices him looking at her.

"You are very hungry, Signor Gabriele?"

"Very hungry, Mother Superior. Very hungry, indeed. I have not really eaten for almost two days." Dante almost chokes on his food as he answers.

She smiles and Dante can see what at one time must have been a beautiful woman. Although he tries to guess her age, he finds it difficult as she is wearing a headdress which leaves very little of her face on display.

"Please continue, Signor Gabriele. I like to see a hungry man eat. There is something almost animal about it."

"I am sorry. I appear to have left my table manners back in my room."

He indicates the array of dishes on the table.

"You seem to eat very well, Mother Superior. This is the best food I have tasted for a long time, probably since I left my family home."

"Yes, we have some able members of the order."

Still putting more food on his plate, Dante nods in agreement.

"They are talented indeed, as if they are trained in the art of good cooking."

Another slight smile crossed the nuns face.

"They are."

"And the silence? No-one is speaking."

"Did your friend Antonio not explain this order to you?"

"No."

The Mother Superior waves her hand to indicate the nuns at their tables, all of whom are eating, but not a word is spoken.

"We are a silent order. Except for prayers, I am the only one who is allowed to speak, and only when it is necessary."

"Ah, that would explain the notes."

"You, of course, can speak to them during your tutorials, but they will not answer. If they have a query they will convey it to you via me."

Dante nods as he puts another forkful of food into his mouth.

"It would be very acceptable for all of us if you were able to play a short hymn before we retire."

"When do you retire?"

"Immediately you have finished eating. We will have a prayer of thanks. Usually we go to our cells to pray for an hour or so but tonight, as you are here, we can take some other thoughts with us."

As she says this, she turns to look directly at him and at the same time gives him a sweet smile.

Reaching out she puts her hand on top of his. The move takes him by surprise.

"Please do not feel the need to hurry with your meal, Signor Gabriele. We are not impatient and will happily wait for you."

This pleases Dante and removing his hand from underneath hers, he reaches out to put some fruit on a side plate. Then he notices that all of the nuns in the hall have finished eating. They are sitting with hands clasped on their laps and looking at the table. Two other nuns are silently removing all signs of the meal.

"It would appear that your ….em…....."

Dante hesitates, looking for the right word. The Mother Superior helps him.

"…..Sisters?"

"Yes, thank you. Sisters. It appears that they are ready now."

He puts some fruit to one side.

"I can finish this later."

As he speaks, a nun he has not even noticed moves behind him and at a discreet nod from the Mother Superior removes his plate, carefully leaving the fruit.

The violin case is at the end of the table and Dante opens it. Taking his time, he carefully polishes the wood with a little cloth which he then places on his shoulder and begins the ritual of tuning the instrument. The sound echoes around the room but nothing makes any of the nuns look up towards him.

When he is happy with the tuning, he places the violin on his shoulder and turns to the Mother Superior.

"I will play some hymns my uncle, a priest, taught me. You may not be familiar with them, but I feel they are appropriate for this occasion."

Without waiting for comment, Dante launches into what could be described as a medley of hymns, gliding from one to the other with effortless skill, as he had done so many times in the past.

It is difficult to gauge the reaction of the audience as they show no sign of any emotion or pleasure as the music sweeps around the large room. The Mother Superior is the only one to show any appreciation at all and it consists of a slight smile on her face and tightly closed eyes.

He plays almost non-stop for about fifteen minutes and brings the short concert to an end with a slow sweet piece that was always favoured by the Ebosta congregation. He stops and slowly lowers the bow and removes the violin from his shoulder. No-one moves. The Mother Superior emerging from her self-induced trance bows slightly to Dante, who bows back. She then sharply claps her hands, just once, but the effect is almost magical.

Instantly every nun stands up, looks straight at Dante and then bows. After a second or two they begin to silently file out. It takes just a couple of minutes for the room to be entirely vacated except for the two at the top table.

A silence settles in the big hall. Dante waits for the Mother Superior to speak to him. He waits as she just sits and stares at the now empty room. Then without warning she rises, walks around the table to face Dante.

"That was a very moving recital, Signor Gabriele. Music can revive many deeply hidden memories."

She looks intently into his eyes and smiles.

"Thank you."

Dante is embarrassed by her close attention and averts his eyes. She speaks again.

"We break our fast at six in the morning. You may join us if you wish. We have our duties to carry out after that and then your pupils will be ready for you at eight. Does that suit your arrangements?"

"Yes, perfectly. How many will there be?"

"We have eight sisters who display some musical abilities, but they are from all levels of competence. Be gentle with them, Signor Gabriele. They are not used to being addressed by a man."

She looks away as she continues.

"Well, not recently."

"That will not be a problem, Mother Superior. They will each progress at their own pace."

She nods to him and then turns to go.

"When can I have my own clothes back?"

"I am told they are still damp from the washing. It may take some time. Are you not comfortable in your surplice?"

The Mother Superior smiles slightly.

"It does become you, Signor Gabriele."

"Yes, very comfortable. I am just not used to such loose clothing; nowhere to put my hands."

He holds them up and gives a short laugh

"Really, your friend Signor Antonio seemed to have few problems with that. He always asked for a surplice as soon as he arrived. I will see you in the morning, Signor Gabriele, God willing. The tuition will take place in this room."

She has now reached the main doorway and leaves without looking back. Dante sits and ponders her words about Antonio when a nun enters the room and begins to douse the candles using a metal cap on a long stick. He mumbles a thank you to her as he now hurriedly leaves the room. The nun totally ignores him.

The sparsely lit corridor is quiet as he makes his way back to his small room. The door is open when he arrives. Inside a candle has been lit and a small bundle is on the bed. He picks it up and it unrolls to reveal another surplice. He holds this one up against himself and discovers it is longer than the one he is wearing

He closes the door, places the new garment on the chair and without undressing slides into the narrow cot. It takes just a few moments after he has blown out the candle for him to fall into a deep exhausted sleep.

Chapter 48

As Dante sleeps peacefully in his mountain nunnery, the rain in Venice is still heavy and Giacomo Grande pulls his cloak around him as he stands in the doorway to his lodgings.

He has been waiting for a let up in the downpour, but after waiting longer than his patience can tolerate, he decides to make a dash for the other side of the narrow alley and take shelter in another deep doorway.

Pulling his felt hat down onto his head he sprints across the road, hopping over the deeper puddles.

He makes it to the other side and curses to himself as he feels the cold water enter his light shoes and begin to soak his silk stockings. He is almost unaware of the other traveller who is also taking shelter in the doorway.

This man has been there for some time and appears to be dry. Giacomo peers out, looking upwards for any sign of the rain easing. The man behind him moves forward and taps the little man on the shoulder. Giacomo steps aside, thinking the man wants to continue on his journey. As he does so, the man punches him in the face. Normally Giacomo would have been alert for such an event, but his concern for his spoiled hosiery had distracted him. The blow was short and brutal.

Giacomo falls to the ground, almost unconscious, but aware enough to know his nose is bleeding and that the man is now ripping open his cloak. Within a second, Giacomo's assailant has exposed the dwarf's codpiece and within another second has ripped it from its stitching. For good measure the robber also grabs the small leather purse tucked into Giacomo's belt. The entire episode has taken no more than three seconds.

Still on the floor and vainly trying to get up, Giacomo feebly utters an oath at the back of the fleeing thief who is now at the far end of the alley.

Chapter 49

The noise is barely perceptible, but such is the silence in the nunnery that it immediately wakes Dante. There is very little light in the room as he investigates the source of the slight scratching.

Thinking it might be a mouse, he leans over and looks under his cot. Peering carefully along the bottom of the wall, his gaze finishes up underneath the door. A sliver of light barely shines through, but what arouses Dante's interest is the fact that it is flickering.

As he watches the noise abruptly stops at the same time as the light goes out.

He flops back onto the pillow and gazes at the ceiling; then he remembers the fruit he took from the dining hall.

Reaching out to the chair where he had left it, he fumbles until he finds the apple. His first bite into the crispy fruit is like a distant canon fire. There is almost an echo along the corridor outside. He takes another bite. The same thing happens. Dante begins to laugh. He has never been in a place so quiet.

He begins to chomp through the fruit and imagines what the Mother Superior would make of noisy apples. He is soon to find out.

The knock on the door stops him chewing, but he has a mouthful of half eaten apple which almost chokes him as he answers the knock.

"Yes?"

He does not really expect a reply but looks to the bottom of the door expecting the inevitable note to appear. He is slightly startled when the Mother Superior answers in a loud whisper.

"If you wish to join us to break your fast we are assembled in the dining hall."

He half sits up in bed.

"Yes. Thank you. I will be there shortly, Mother Superior. Please do not delay on my account."

He listens intently and then hears the same noise as the one that woke him. It dawns on him that it must be the sound of slippers on the stone floor. The sound he had heard was obviously the Sisters making their way to the hall. The noise fades away as he gets out of bed. The water in the wash jug is icy cold and he plunges his hands into it to wash his face.

Taking off the surplice he has worn all night he dries himself with it and suddenly realises how cold it is to stand there naked in this stone cell. He pulls the clean surplice over his head and adjusts the tight collar around his neck.

Opening the door slowly he sees there is no-one in the corridor. He tries to remember the route to the dining hall and has to almost grope his way along the corridor which is now void of candles to guide him. He eventually finds himself outside the large wooden doors. In spite of their size, they swing open easily as he gently pushes at them.

All of the nuns are back where they were at dinner the previous evening except now they are all standing, hands held in front of them and with the same downward cast eyes.

The Mother Superior is also standing. She smiles at him slightly as he makes his way towards her. Before he reaches her table, which is again set for just two people, she claps her hands just once and the nuns immediately sit down and two more emerge from a side door with trays of food.

As Dante sits, a small bowl of grain and a jug of milk is placed in front of him and this is followed by another plate with some fruit and two small bread buns. As he looks around the room, it appears that everyone is eating the same food.

Mother Superior turns to him.

"We gave thanks while we waited for you, Signor Gabriele. I presume you gave thanks before joining us?"

Dante is pouring some milk onto his bowl of grain when she asks him this question. He stops in mid pour.

"Thanks?"

She looks at his bowl of grain. "For the food."

Nodding vigorously he continues pouring the milk.

"Of course, yes. Before I had my fruit from last night."

Smiling at his answer she begins to eat.

"We will be taking your tuition in a short while. The more talented sisters will have instruments but the rest will watch and hopefully be inspired by both your music and your teaching."

The spartan meal is soon over and the nuns once again resume their pose, their hands on their laps; the two nuns clear the dishes.

Dante is having trouble swallowing the rough grain in his bowl. This may also be because he has a very dry throat. It is a relief to him when he sees the Mother Superior put down her spoon and gently push her dish away .

Dante pushes his plate away too and rises. Already the nuns are transforming the seating arrangements in the room and eight chairs are placed at the front in a small semicircle. A single chair is placed some feet away facing them.

Dante swallows hard as he views the seating arrangement. It looks like a trial scenario and he is the accused.

Turning to the Mother Superior he mumbles.

"I will go and get my violin. I may be some moments so it would be good if the pupils could spend time tuning their instruments."

She nods in approval and makes her way to the front of the hall as he quickly exits and dashes to his room.

Dante slams shut the door when he arrives. There is still no sign of his clothes. Sitting on the bed he opens the violin case and carries out his normal ritual of polishing and tuning. When he can polish and tune no longer he puts the instrument away again and takes some sheet music from his bag.

Bracing himself, he opens the door and with the air of someone walking to the gallows and trying not to look craven about it, he strides manfully, as manfully as he can in a long surplice, along the corridor.

The usual silence greets him as he enters the hall. All of the nuns are now facing him. Dante sits on his chair and then gets up again. He nervously begins to thumb through his sheet music and selects a short piece which he puts on the stand.

Turning and moving towards the assembly, he begins to address them.

"Good morning, everyone. I am pleased to be here and I look forward to some pleasant hours of music, music played on one of the finest instruments ever created."

There is a complete silence.

"I will begin by playing a short piece and then we can all play it one at a time in order to assess your abilities."

He smiles at the eight pupils. They do not respond.

The Mother Superior takes up her position at the back of the hall. It takes a little while for him to realise she is in the room and when he does his nervousness reaches new heights. He accidentally flicks his bow at the sheet music in the stand which scatters across the floor.

As he bends down to gather up the paper he thinks he hears a little snigger of laughter from one of the nuns. He turns to look but they are all still stony faced. He carries on picking up the paper and hears it again.

The Mother Superior also hears it and stands up. The sniggering stops.

As Dante sits, so does the Mother Superior. The room is totally silent as he begins to play the first notes. The piece is not long and he knows it off by heart. After a while he takes his eyes off the sheet music to see if there is any reaction from his audience.

The facial expressions on the nuns at the back are the same and there is an intensity on the faces of his pupils. He also notices they are not sitting as upright as they were before.

One or two of the pupils are positively slouching in their chairs and behind them several nuns are apparently adjusting their clothing.

Dante returns to the sheet music. After a number of pages he looks again.

He almost drops the bow at what he sees.

Chapter 50

As usual the bullock does not want to be where Franco wants it to be. It really wants to move over to the hedgerow and eat what looks like juicy green grass. The thick mud in the wet field is not too attractive to the animal and it tugs Franco with him as he pulls on the stout hemp rope.

The other animal in the field watches with just the modicum of interest. Tessy the donkey is already tethered to the fence and is happily chewing on some damp hay as she watches the struggle between man and beast. The rain starts again as the bullock reaches the hedgerow and stops pulling on the rope as it begins to eat.

Franco, now in a thoroughly foul mood, walks back to the donkey and takes a stout stick from the raffia carrier on its back. The bullock seems to ignore the first whack on its buttocks and continues eating. The second whack from the stick is much harder and now Franco has its almost undivided attention as, still chewing, it slowly turns to regard him.

Picking up another rope, Franco swings it across the broad back of the animal. Now he has two ropes attached and the other end he takes across to the half exposed roots of the large oak tree that fell some days ago.

All of the branches have been moved and the rest cut up for fire wood. These were stacked in a neat pile which Bruno is loading onto a low wagon. They will be taken back to a dry barn at the farm.

Lying beside this stack of timber are three small olive trees with their roots tied up in wet sacking. They are going to be the replacement for the once mighty oak. But first the roots have to be removed. That's where the bullock comes in.

Franco had tried using Tessy the donkey but she made absolutely no impression on the tree root and soon lost enthusiasm, in spite of his frantic and then sweet urgings. She was just too old and frail.

In a towering bad mood, Franco had used his broad bladed axe to chop away at the thick and deeply embedded roots before accepting the fact that he would have to use the bullock. The bullock resisted being dragged from its warm byre and fought against both Franco and his son as they forced it up the hill.

Franco walks over to Bruno who is struggling with the loading of the heavier logs.

"Bruno, go and get the priest. Tell him we need an extra pair of hands, his hands."

Bruno hesitates.

"He will be in the middle of saying mass. Do you want me to disturb him?"

"Yes, Bruno. That is exactly what I want you to do. He made a promise and now it is time to start keeping it. His God has eternal life and can wait; we have until the heavy weather arrives and can't wait. Now go."

Bruno unties his leather apron and begins to walk down the hillside as Franco settles down on a log and tries to light the damp tobacco in his pipe.

Arriving at the church, Bruno slowly pushes open the large doors and peers in. His uncle is indeed in the middle of taking mass, but he immediately spots his young nephew beckoning to him through the partly opened door. Without hesitation he nods that he understands and carries on with giving out the small communion wafers. Bruno silently closes the door.

Chapter 51

To the right of Dante's small group of student nuns, the two on the extreme edge have managed to raise their surplices and are now revealing their thighs. Unlike the surplice Dante is wearing, theirs seem to be able to open at the front. As he plays and watches, they begin to open their legs. Dante misses a couple of notes as he breaks out in a sweat. The nuns keep staring straight at him as they carry on.

Dante casts a quick glance in the direction of the Mother Superior. She is sitting with her hands clasped on her lap and has her eyes closed.

Now the nuns directly in front of Dante are begin to open their surplices. He plays on. Sweat now trickles down his face. He turns the sheet music. He is near the end of the piece and will have to stand up and approach the nearest pupil.

Only one thing is going to stop him. He has an erection and it is becoming obvious. Without the constriction of his breeches, Dante's penis is now slowly raising the heavy material of the surplice. He reaches the end of the piece.

The Mother Superior opens her eyes and smiles at him, then closes them again. He smiles back but she doesn't seem to register as she appears to have entered her trance like state again.

Dante sits transfixed. With all his might he is willing his penis to subside. He cannot possibly stand up like this. He could cover the tumescence with his violin, but it would be obvious to anyone who cared to look that he had a problem.

He shuffles his sheet music again, bending over more than is normal and then he clears his throat to speak.

"Perhaps that piece was a little too short. I will now play a longer piece in order for all of us to appreciate some of the fine variations that a violin can register within the grouping of a large orchestra."

Even he knows he is speaking nonsense but he places a number of sheets on the stand. He still has his problem. Fearfully he casts a look at the pupils.

Four of them were now openly displaying their vaginas, legs apart and the surplice splayed to either side. Two were shaved and the others were covered in a thick mass of pubic hair.

Dante is speechless.

One of the nuns closes her legs and then opens them again, slowly.

His penis responds by jerking. This is noticed by the nuns who never stop staring at him. But for the first time it brings a slight smile to their faces.

Other nuns are undoing the top of their surplices and baring their breasts. All in complete silence.

Grabbing his violin case and violin which he places in front of his crutch as cover, he suddenly rises and dashes for the door. As he moves across the open space to reach it he notices the Mother Superior is not present in the room.

Pushing the door open he is aware of movement in the hall behind him. The nuns are beginning to get up and follow him. He slams the door and runs along the corridor to his room.

He reaches the first corner and looks behind him when a pair of strong hands suddenly reach out from a doorway and drag him in. He is bundled into a darkened room and pushed against the wall. His abductor slowly closes the door and leans against it.

After a few moments there is a sound in the corridor. It is the sound of many slipper clad feet moving rapidly past the door.

The shuffling feet take several seconds to pass by and when it goes silent the Mother Superior raises her hand and places a finger on her lips. A sign for Dante to stay silent.

They both stare at each other in the gloom. There is a noise outside the door. Someone has been listening. The sound of the feet quietly moving away allows the Mother Superior to relax her hand and she leads Dante to one of two chairs in the corner of the room.

Sitting opposite him she again signals for silence.

Chapter 52

The rain is still heavy and the wind is strong, but it helps Father Emanuele walk up the hill to his brother. His wide black cassock is billowing out like a ship's sail and pushes him along. He is slightly breathless when he arrives at the little wet group gathered at the old oak stump.

The bullock is still chewing grass and the donkey is huddling closer to it to avoid the rain. Both animals are now adorned with ropes and harnesses which Bruno is making secure, and he leads them back to the old tree stump

"We could have picked a more clement day to do this brother," the priest says as he arrives.

Franco nods at him.

"Aye, we could."

He looks up at the dark clouds.

"Why don't you have a word with someone?"

The good natured priest laughs.

"No doubt he would listen, but I fear he will be getting more important messages today than a couple of old dogs wanting the rain to stop."

"A glass of wine and some cheese would suffice so tell him to put it over yonder. We can have it when we are finished. Not too much to ask, is it?"

"Far too much and he is not a waiter!"

Franco hands Emanuele one of the ropes.

"What is the point of having a brother as a priest if we cannot get any special service?"

Emanuele walks around the head of the bullock and leads the rope through a metal ring on the harness.

"Maybe we could just ask for a little help in getting this stump out then we can get back to your wife's warm kitchen."

He looks across at Franco.

"Always seems to be plenty of wine and cheese there."

"Aye, and all provided by me."

As he says this he hits the bullock on the hindquarters and the big animal reluctantly begins to pull the rope tight. Emanuele and Bruno both pull at the donkey's harness. Nothing seems to make any difference.

"You take the bullock," Franco says as he picks up the axe and begins to walk to the base of the root, "and I will hack at it until it gives. Just keep the animal pulling."

The rain gets heavier as the little group sets about their back-breaking task.

Emanuele's feet slip in the mud and he stumbles slightly onto one of his knees. His black cassock is now wearing a dark brown patch, which he makes bigger by trying to rub it off. Franco notices this and gives a little smile as he smashes the axe into a thick, dark, gnarled root.

Chapter 53

Dante and the Mother Superior sit in silence, both listening intently for any signs of movement outside in the corridor. He looks around the room which is large and comfortably furnished. A log fire burns in a wide fireplace and the walls are lined with full bookcases. A few minutes pass before she speaks, almost in a whisper.

"I must beg your forgiveness, Signor Gabriele."

He looks at her as she continues.

"I thought you knew."

"Knew what?"

She leans across and takes his hand.

"About the order. Who we are and why we are here."

He shakes his head.

"I came to teach music."

"Is that what Antonio told you? Just to teach music? That is all?"

Dante considers before answering.

"Well, he never told me anything. We just got a note with the details. He could not come and he asked if I could take over for him. We needed the money, so I said yes."

She places a hand on Dante's.

"The sisters here are not all following a religious life. Some were placed here by cruel, heartless families, because they were girls."

She smiles at him.

"Who needs girls? Dowries are very expensive and it takes away a family's wealth. Much better to have boys. A number came here to escape the world. And they have. Here they will stay."

She pauses.

"How is Luisa?"

Dante is both shocked and surprised as she says this and it stuns him into a silence.

"Antonio told me you were living together."

"Yes, we are. But how do you know Luisa? Did she come here to teach? She never mentioned it."

Dante is feeling slightly stunned.

The Mother Superior gets up and walks to the glass paneled door which leads out onto a wide stone terrace. She is silent for a few moments as she looks out. Then she turns to him.

"Yes, Luisa did play here."

Dante shakes his head slightly.

"Then why did she not say?"

"She played here as a nun."

The impact of this remark is a total shock to Dante. He just stares at her.

"She was a nun, sent here by her father when she was a young girl. Antonio came here to give some tuition and met her. He took her away when he left. He has done that several times. The younger nuns see it as a way to move away from here. The ones who are not talented, or old and ugly, are destined to stay here in this place until they die."

The realisation dawns slowly on Dante.

"That is why they did what they did? Displayed themselves?"

Her silence answers his question.

"Then Luisa must have done that with Antonio."

Again silence. He holds his head in his hands pushing the balls of his thumbs into his eyes in an attempt to blank out the images.

Eventually, he looks up at her.

"Were you abandoned by your father, too?"

She laughs and shakes her head.

"No, it was not my father who abandoned me. I never knew him. It was my lover, the father of my child, who abandoned me."

She waits a moment and then speaks again, quietly.

"He is a nobleman who took me into his home as a young girl. We were very happy. I became pregnant and his family told him it was not acceptable. One week after the baby was born I was brought here, many years ago."

"That is a worse betrayal. Why did you not leave?"

"Leave?"

She ponders for a while.

"Leave to go where? In this place the nuns took care of me. Over time I became one of them and then eventually their leader."

She indicates the room.

"I am safe, fed, looked after and respected."

"Your child. What became of your baby?"

"A boy. I was told he died, soon after he was taken from me."

"I'm sorry."

"Don't be. It happened a long time ago. I accept my life here and will probably die in this place."

Dante stands up.

"That is also sad. You can leave. Come with me."

She smiles at him.

"Thank you, but I have planned my life and I am happy here."

She suddenly changes her tone, as if she wants to end that conversation.

"But *you* must leave soon. It will be difficult for you here now."

She points to a small pile of clothes on the desk.

"Your clothes. Put them on and then come out onto the terrace with me. I want you to play just once more before you leave."

Dante hurriedly grabs the clothes and begins to remove his surplice. The Mother Superior turns away and uses a large key to unlock the door to the stone terrace.

Dropping the heavy garment to the floor, Dante stands for a moment completely naked as he fumbles in the gloom to sort out his clothes. He is suddenly aware of the Mother

Superior looking at him from the doorway. He pulls a shirt in front of his crutch to hide himself.

The nun keeps looking and then moves her hand in a downwards motion. Dante slowly lets the shirt fall to the floor.

She continues to stare at him. Only a few feet separates them but Dante can feel the intensity of her look as she lets her eyes roam across his body. He finds it strangely erotic, with the inevitable consequence: his erection begins to grow. She sees it and concentrates her gaze on his now almost fully erect penis.

A slight smile crosses her face and she looks him in the eye.

"One thing the rest of the order and I have in common is the love of a man's body. Thank you for showing me yours. Luisa is not only beautiful, but a very fortunate woman. Now please join me and play some music."

With a swift final glance at his erection, she turns and walks out onto the terrace.

Dante dons his clothes as quickly as he can and taking his violin he walks out behind her. The Mother Superior has moved across the wide terrace and is now standing at the edge looking out into the dark valley below. She beckons to him to join her.

The wall around the terrace is low and castellated and the drop from it is sheer. Dante carefully peers over as the Mother Superior points out the small river that runs along the valley floor a thousand feet below them.

"It is rumoured that when the Monks lived here that one or two went to meet their maker by stepping off this wall." She pats the granite slab she is leaning on.

Dante takes a step back.

"I always thought that suicide was a mortal sin. No heaven."

She turns to him.

"I feel that sometimes it is justified, for instance, when one can no longer suffer this world. God is supposed to be all forgiving and he could hardly deny entry to a devoted follower." She smiles as she walks to the centre of the terrace.

"Now please play for me before you depart, Signor Gabriele."

Dante points to the building which towers above them. "The Sisters?"

She holds up her key ring.

"They cannot enter this area. It is only for me. I have bolted the inner door. You are safe here."

With a quick glance towards the upper windows, Dante begins to play. The Mother Superior turns her back to him and seems to be in prayer as she holds her hands in front of her. He can see her shoulders moving slightly. The music he is playing is sombre and he changes it to something livelier. This seems to change her mood and she slowly starts to move in a circle.

Chapter 54

The field is now very muddy from the constant rain and Emanuele has difficulty keeping his feet as he pulls at the harness of the bullock with Bruno desperately urging the donkey.

Franco is still frantically hacking away at the roots of the tree in what is rapidly becoming a mud filled hole.

He keeps shouting at his brother after every whack with the axe as he tries to separate the deep and stubborn roots from the large stump of the tree.

"Pull, Priest. Pull."

Emanuele just grits his teeth, swallows the insult and smiles as Bruno grins at him and shrugs his shoulders. His only thought is that with some more effort this dreadful day will soon be over and he will be safely back in his small abode at the rear of his church.

He urges the animal to greater effort, continually slipping as he does so.

Chapter 55

Slowly the Mother Superior holds out her arms sideways and without even glancing at him she begins to spin.

Dante sensing the moment begins to play a little faster. The nun responds and is moving around the terrace, arms akimbo as she whirls around the large space. He plays a little faster and now she is whirling quite fast.

He is aware of a noise above his head, a slight murmuring, and still playing he looks up. There are four windows cut into the granite face of the monastery and every piece of space is taken up by the faces of the nuns as they watch their Mother Superior dancing to a wild gypsy tune.

Dante carefully backs up against the low wall. The Mother Superior is now spinning madly around the terrace, her surplice begins to rise on the force of her turns; it rises higher as she continues to whirl ever faster. Then Dante sees her bare white buttocks as she spins past him, her dress rises still more as she moves to the outer wall and Dante can now see her bare from the waist down.

The nun seems lost in her own world as she moves even faster, her dress almost horizontal as she turns.

Dante is mesmerized by the sight of her bare body as she whirls past him. He plays even faster as she spirals away across the stone flagstones and then she suddenly stops, her surplice drops down again and with a quivering finger she points out over the wall into the valley.

Dante stops playing and turns to see what it is she is pointing at. There is nothing to see except the yawning space beyond the wall. The shuffle of feet on the stone floor slabs of the terrace make him swing back to see the contorted face of the Mother Superior as she rushes towards him. Her voice is shrill as she runs at him with her outstretched hands clawing at him.

"You will not have them. They are mine."

She is almost upon him, clearly intent on pushing him over the wall. He rapidly steps to one side. Her foot hits the small step up to the wall and she stumbles. Her clutching fingers narrowly miss his face as she falls past him.

Instinctively raising the bow to protect himself it slides between the nuns neck and her crucifix chain. The chain snaps and wraps itself around the bow. The Mother Superior suddenly realises she cannot be saved and with a half scream she tumbles over the edge of the wall.

Within a moment she has disappeared.

The only sound he hears at first is from the soft wind that sings through the branches of the tall pines on the mountainside. Then another sound intervenes. It is the soft mewing of calves when their mother is not there to feed them. The sound is low and constant.

He realises it is coming from the nuns in the window spaces above his head. Still in shock he looks back to the low wall where the nun has fallen and suddenly a large white bird appears. It swoops and dives and swoops some more.

It takes a moment or two for Dante to see it is the Mother Superior's white wimple that has obviously been torn from her head as she plummeted to her death.

The headdress makes one last twist and then follows its mistress in a steep dive and out of Dante's view.

Chapter 56

The face makes a squelchy sound as it crashes into the soft wet earth. The mud is forced through the teeth and into the open mouth that is stretched wide in a gasp of agony.

Father Emanuele Gabriele is dead a moment before he hits the ground as a massive heart attack instantly deprives him of his life.

Unnoticed by Bruno, the priest lays there in the muddy slime and both bullock and donkey try to avoid him as they struggle through the thick mud and past his now completely lifeless body.

Father Emanuele does not hear the cry of triumph from his brother who has at last managed to remove the roots of the old oak tree from its deep base.

Chapter 57

Pulling on his jacket and running as fast as he can along the corridor holding his violin case tightly, Dante can hear the shuffling sound of slippers behind him. There is no sign of the nuns but the idea of them moving somewhere behind him is scaring him to death.

He had been rooted to the spot staring at where the Mother Superior had fallen; his trance had been broken by the sound of sobbing from the windows above, followed by shrieks and screams.

And then the most frightening thing that can happen in a silent order of nuns: the screaming of the words "Get him!"

Realising that he is the object of their intention, he runs even faster.

The massive wooden door is bolted and he looks for anything that might get it open. In his panic he fails to realise that the bolt just needs to be slid back in its cradle for the door to open.

The nuns could only be a matter of some yards behind him now. He turns and there they are, at the bottom of the steps leading up to the dormitory from where they had seen the incident.

He stops and puts his back to the door.

They also stop and as usual they just stare at him. Some of the nuns are naked and some bare breasted. All of them look angry and in some form of distress.

An older, small nun, whose surplice is hanging from her bare shoulders, suddenly lurches forward and begins to sprint towards him.

Dante realises his life could soon be over and he spins around, accidentally catching the sliding bolt with his elbow. The door slips slightly ajar. It is enough, and moving as if the very devil is behind him, Dante pushes through the gap and out onto the gravel track that leads to the relative safety of the forest.

Still running as fast as he can he reaches the top of the track and stops to look back at the monastery.

There is no-one to be seen, but there is still the keening sound of souls in torment.

Almost at once the windows above the doorway begin to fill up with faces, lots of faces, again all staring at him. Every stone framed window is crammed with small white faces as he turns and begins running away.

The sound of the wailing follows him as he dashes as fast as he can into the dark forest.

Chapter 58

Several days later

Luisa's face is swollen and her eyes are puffy as Dante helps her away from the large earthenware pot where she has just vomited. She sits on the edge of the bed with her head between her hands. Once again her hair is wet with sweat but this time passion is not the cause.

After a few seconds she leans forward and vomits some more. Dante watches from just beside her and as she sits up again he offers her a towel to wipe her face. Taking the towel she slowly wipes and then turns to look at him.

"And then there were three. Mr. Farmer's boy, I thought you knew how to prevent these things on a farm."

Dante nods.

"It's easy on a farm. You keep the male animals locked away from the females."

She gives a little snort.

"Maybe we should give that idea some more thought. Try it out here."

A smile crosses his face.

"Impossible! On a farm there is no animal as pretty as you."

Luisa shakes her head and then quickly revisits the pot and vomits some more. Sitting up again she takes hold of Dante's hand.

"I cannot play like this. You will have to earn some more money to keep us."

Gently he puts his arm around her shoulder.

"Of course, and for the marriage. My uncle will marry us in his church."

She gently pushes him away.

"There will be no marriage just yet."

Thinking she is joking he carries on.

"A baby must have parents and a good family home."

Luisa gives a little bitter laugh.

"Dante I am not going to live on your father's farm, wherever it is. Ever. I am not a farm girl. You will have to get more regular work. I will teach you some of the more difficult pieces for the quartets and Antonio will help by getting you work with some of the ensembles."

She takes his hand and kisses his palm.

"It is so nice having you back with me so early even though it took the death of the Mother Superior to bring it about. What a stupid, tragic way to die, tripping and falling like that. You were only gone a few days but it felt like eternity."

She stares intently into his eyes.

"Promise me you will never leave me alone again?"

Dante smiles in agreement and as she rolls back onto the bed he gently lifts her feet up and then covers her with a blanket. He wipes the sweat from her face and leans over to kiss her. She stops him.

"No, Dante. I must sleep now."

He looks intently into her eyes.

"We have to talk about Antonio, and you. He sent me to that terrible place where he found you. He still goes there; still takes girls away."

She smiles weakly.

"I know, Dante. He tells me all about it. He helps them find a new life, like he did with me."

"Where does he take them? Are they all musicians? Do you know any of them?"

"No, and I do not want to. There are too many bad memories of that place."

Reaching into his jacket pocket, Dante pulls out the broken crucifix chain from the Mother Superior and hands it to her.

"I fancy that there will be no more unfortunate girls being locked away there. This was torn from her as she stumbled over the wall."

Even as he tells the lie about what happened, he feels guilty.

"I tried to save her."

Luisa takes the black stone crucifix with a silver figure of Jesus embedded into it and looks at him.

"It's the symbol of her office; only she can wear it."

Dante rubs his finger over the crucifix.

"She doesn't need it anymore."

"I still cannot believe she fell from that terrace, Dante. I have not been able to get the picture of it from my head since you told me."

He almost whispers the words.

"It was an accident. She was dancing, twirling; she must have become dizzy and lost her balance."

He looks at her intently.

"Do you think she meant to fall, to kill herself? She said something as she stumbled, about me not having them. Do you know what she meant?"

She takes the small crucifix from him and then turns away as she answers.

"Questions, Dante. Too many questions. We can talk about it later. Right now I am both tired and hungry. Please go and get me something nice to eat, for when I wake up."

She turns back to him and smiles before slowly closing her eyes. Within moments she is fast asleep.

Dante watches her for a little while and then creeps quietly to the door.

Chapter 59

The stall holder passes over the string bag of oranges and plums to Dante who then moves across the narrow alley to look at a fish stall. Another purchase as two small but fat fish are wrapped and dropped into the bag. The market area is strung out along a very narrow passageway and the crowd jostle each other as they move along. A tall man dressed entirely in black with a scarf concealing his face and standing several stalls away briefly peers at Dante and after a moment or two merges into the crowd.

Another purchase at the bread stall and Dante puts the freshly baked loaf into the string bag. Pushing his way through the crowd he feels a tug on his jacket. Fearing a pick pocket, he swings round to see a small man, almost a dwarf, looking up at him.

"Are you Dante, the musician?" the small man asks as he takes a step back, noticing the look on Dante's face.

"My name is Dante, and I play a violin, so it could be me. Who asks?"

The small man takes a step nearer and thrusts a creased piece of paper into Dante's hand.

"Friend of Giacomo's."

He steps away again.

"Typical full grown, no respect for us little uns. I have been trying to catch up with you since you left your building. Do you have to move so fast?"

Dante shrugs his shoulders.

"Sorry, I will try to slow down next time I walk out, just in case someone with short legs wants to talk to me!"

Ignoring Dante's remark the small man points to the note.

"He said you would pay me for delivering that."

"That was very generous of him."

"Aren't you gonna read it then?"

A slightly amused Dante unfurls the piece of paper and scans the note which briefly says, *Dear friend, I must see you now. In mortal danger. The rear door at the Palazzo Rialto. Giacomo.'*
Dante bends down to the little man's face level.
"What's wrong with him?"
"He was robbed and beaten. He's in a very bad way."
Dante looks at the note again then back to the small man.
"My lodgings, you know where they are."
He holds out the bag of food.
"I will pay you double if you deliver these to the top floor room, to a Luisa Bazzo. Tell her I will be back soon."
He holds out a coin which the little man snaffles quickly, grabs the bag and disappears into the crowd. Dante watches until he is sure the man is going in the right direction and then turns to make his way to the Rialto Bridge.

Chapter 60

The Palazzo Rialto is a massive building by Venetian standards. It was once home to a family from Genoa who fell on hard times when the father gambled most of their wealth away; his two sons turned the grand building into a hostelry. It stands on the Grand Canal and is one of the most popular venues for the local population of the city. The canal entrance is always busy with gondolas and private vessels dropping off their clients. At the side entrance the alley is just wide enough to accommodate all of the deliveries that a large hostelry needs on a daily basis.

It takes Dante almost thirty minutes to walk across town, but eventually he arrives at the side entrance to push and weave his way through dozens of men with barrows waiting to have their deliveries checked in and signed for. The man in charge of the delivery team is tall and muscular with a shaven head and a number of scars on his face. He stands on a small box at the entrance barking out orders to both the delivery men and the hostelry porters who hustle the goods into the cavernous hall where they are stored before being distributed to the various departments.

Dante attempts to catch the overseer's eye but the man is concentrating on making sure the goods he has signed for are delivered inside. After a few moments of ineffectually waving at him, Dante suddenly lets out a huge bellow.

"Giacomo Grande."

His voice manages to rise above the general noise level and the overseer looks at him.

"You Dante?"

Dante nods. The man indicates with his hand for him to come forward.

When Dante is close enough, the man bends down and whispers in his ear, "Giacomo is in a private room. Just a moment."

Standing to his full, considerable height, the man claps his hands three times and the noise level both inside the hallway and outside just simply stops. The man points to a young girl in a maid's uniform who is loitering just inside the entrance.

"You there."

The girl is suddenly rigid with embarrassment as everyone looks at her.

"Take this gentleman to Signor Grande's quarters. Immediately."

The girl looks scared but beckons Dante to follow her. He squeezes past the overseer and runs to catch up as she moves into the unlit interior and along a dark corridor. At the bottom of a wide wooden staircase she stops and turns to him.

"Sir, I do not wish to go any further but the person you seek is up these steps. Turn right and it is the second doorway on the left."

With that she hurries away back down the corridor.

Dante watches her go and wonders briefly why she seems so scared. He looks up the wooden staircase and then slowly begins to climb. At the top he follows her instructions and turns right.

The passage way is dimly lit with only small windows open at each end. He reaches the second doorway on the left and listens for a moment. Hearing nothing he raises his hand to knock when the door suddenly bursts open and another young woman pushes her way out of the room. She is clutching her long dress around her thighs and trying to make herself decent. Barely noticing Dante, she turns and hisses back into the dark interior.

"You pervert. That is the last time, and here's me trying to give you some sympathy. You can starve to death for all I care."

Adjusting her clothing she gives a scornful look at Dante, wipes a tear from her eye and clutching her dress and petticoats around her she scurries like a scared chicken back to the top of the wooden stairway.

Slowly pushing the door open, he peers into the gloom. Spotting a large window which is heavily curtained he moves across the room to open the drapes. A weak voice from the darkness stops him.

"Dante, help me. Over here. Don't let any light in. I am too badly beaten to be looked upon."

Looking in the direction of the voice Dante asks, "Giacomo, is that you?"

The voice is much stronger now.

"Of course it is, you fool. Who else would it be? Now close the door and come over here."

Dante closes the door and moves towards the voice. There is a weak shaft of light that shows up a bed. Giacomo suddenly rolls into the light and stands up. He is now almost face to face with Dante. The two men stare at each other.

"Look at me."

Giacomo's voice is almost a whisper again.

"My beauty torn away. I am scarred for life. Who would consider me now?"

Dante scrutinises the dwarf's face. Apart from two small scratches there are no visible signs of bruising.

"You look exactly the same."

This is not the answer that Giacomo is expecting and he changes his whisper into a growl.

"The bruising is inside, Dante. I would expect a sensitive spirit like yours to be able to see that."

He chokes back a little sob.

"The shame of it. My manhood ripped away from me!"

He looks straight into Dante's face.

"*Again!*"

A slightly angry Dante leans close to Giacomo.

"You do realise I left a sick lover to come and see you. I had to send her food with your little friend because I thought you were in mortal danger."

Giacomo falls back onto the pillows.

"Perspective, Dante. Always perspective."

Then his voice hardens.

"Now, who did you tell?"

"About what?"

Giacomo suddenly grabs at his crotch.

"About this."

Dante laughs.

"According to the maids here there seems to be nothing wrong with that."

"Not that. My codpiece. I was attacked by a gang of ruffians who beat me up and stole it. Now, who did you tell?"

The realization of the situation suddenly dawns on Dante and he sits down on the chair at the side of the bed. As he does so Giacomo suddenly gets up onto his knees and slips his stiletto knife between the two of them. Taking hold of Dante by the shirt front, he brings the sharp pointed blade up to the face of the young man.

"If I were to push this into your eyes and slit them, I could not make you more blind than passion has."

Dante says nothing but looks straight at Giacomo as he continues.

"Did you tell your female fiddler?"

Dante shakes his head and Giacomo leans closer.

"What did you do with the diamond I gave you?"

"Sold it. We have been living on the money for the past few months."

Anger begins to creep into Giacomo's voice.

"Then you must have told her where you got it from."

It takes a few moments for Dante to reluctantly agree and then he says quickly.

"Yes, but under solemn promise she would keep it a secret."

Giacomo relaxes a little and even forces a smile onto his face.

"Were you in bed with her at the time?"

Dante lowers his eyes as he knows Giacomo is right once more, and then in a little whiny voice Giacomo questions him again.

"Were you between her legs?"

Now it's Dante's turn to be angry. He grabs Giacomo's wrist and pushes the knife away. Giacomo falls back onto the pillows.

"Enough. She promised she wouldn't tell anyone; she gave her word."

Shaking his head Giacomo gives a little laugh.

"The word of an addict has the value of a contract written in snow."

Dante is quick to react.

"What do you mean, that Luisa is an addict?"

Giacomo ignores the question and props himself up on a pillow.

"You needed money so you sold the stone. Now you need more money, why are you both not working?"

Dante rises and moves to the window. He pulls aside the thick curtain and gazes out.

"Luisa has been ill. We have lost our contact. He has been in Vienna with Mozart's orchestra."

Again Giacomo gives a little snort of disdain.

"Your lost contact would be your friend Antonio, correct? And your female friend is suffering from the vapors no doubt."

Dante turns from the window and looks at him.

Giacomo continues.

"Your very best friend in the world, Antonio, has been here in Venice. He has never left; he has been here entertaining the Countess and supplying her and her gang of imbeciles with the thing they desire most. He is also the thief who stole my diamonds."

Dante shakes his head in denial.

"Impossible, you are such a liar, Giacomo. And you said you were attacked by a gang of ruffians."

"True, I lied. But that was to build sympathy and hide my shame. It felt like a gang and he knew exactly what he was looking for. I could have died if I had put up resistance."

"And what would he supply the Countess with?"

Giacomo smiles to himself.

"Ah, the nub of the matter, Dante. The little green bottles from the Orient that supply the sensations of paradise apparently."

Dante looks at him, not understanding what he is talking about. Giacomo supplies the information.

"Opium."

"Ridiculous, are you saying Luisa is an opium addict?"

"Yes, I am my young friend. Supplied by Antonio, as he supplies most of Venice and has done for years."

An indignant Dante again shakes his head and blurts out, "Luisa is ill because she is pregnant with our child."

This is met with a shrug of Giacomo's shoulder.

"She may well be pregnant but I am willing to wager she is ill because she has been spending your money on this drug."

"No. No. She can't have told Antonio about your diamonds or gotten his drugs because she hasn't seen him recently."

Another casual shrug from Giacomo.

"And she told you that did she?"

"Of course not. I have never had reason to ask her."

A little chuckle from the dwarf.

"In the world of fools and cuckolds, blindness is obviously darker."

Dante turns back to the window and looks out.

Giacomo warms to his subject.

"Her father placed her in a nunnery when she was a child. It is not uncommon among the gentry. He completely abandoned her. At sixteen thanks to Antonio, she was already an addict, to both men and opium. She and Antonio have been lovers for a long time. When she was younger she gave herself as payment, now she is older she needs money and a young man to earn it."

Dante shakes his head in disbelief.

"Antonio told Lorenzo she broke out of a convent and made her way to Venice as young girl. At the nunnery the Mother Superior told me that she left with Antonio after one of his visits."

"Then someone is lying and it is not me."

Giacomo gives a little snort.

"You were no doubt told he had helped others escape, to become musicians."

There is no reaction from Dante and Giacomo continues.

"They may have left the nunnery but they never made it to the musical circle. Antonio used them for himself and then moved them on. You don't have to be even remotely clever to work out where they finished up. Rumour is that he trades them for the drug. They all seem to disappear."

Dante suddenly turns and slides down the wall to sit on the floor. Everything Giacomo is telling him has a ring of truth to it.

"I love her," he mutters, almost to himself,

Giacomo's words drift to him out of the gloom.

"There are as many women in the world as there are as fish in the oceans. All a man has to do is cast a line out. Even stunted and broken creatures such as myself can often land a prize catch and if it is not to your taste then you throw it back and catch another one."

Dante takes his time, not really wanting to ask the question.

"The baby?"

The answer is brutal and stuns him for a short while.

"If there is one, then it is probably not yours."

At this major insult Dante begins to push himself back up the wall. Giacomo casually points his dagger at him.

"Tell me, did she suddenly find herself madly attracted to you, seduce you and keep you locked in that ever so sweet honey trap? Did she?"

This brings no response from Dante as he just leans against the wall, locked in his own thoughts. Giacomo rolls over and props himself up on an elbow.

"Hmm, thought so. God has a lot to answer for. Why did he give everything a man desires to the most treacherous of creatures, a woman?"

"What am I to do, Giacomo?"

Giacomo points to a corner of the room.

"There are several bottles of wine over there. Open them and we can discuss your options as we dull our senses. At least we will be starting from a level base."

Dante gropes his way to a small table in the corner where there are indeed several bottle of wine. He pulls the cork from one and takes two glasses over to the bed. He hands the bottle to Giacomo who gently takes it and a glass from him.

"This is mine, Dante. Go and get another one for yourself. We will need more than one each; we have much to discuss and plan "

Once again and without saying a word, Dante takes a bottle for himself and settles back down on the floor. Both men pour out a measure and quickly drain the glass.

Chapter 61

Across the narrow road from Luisa's lodgings is a small but very busy tavern. Giacomo's friend and messenger is sitting enjoying a glass of wine and the company of a plump older lady who seems to be very friendly with him, squeezing him and kissing him on the cheek.

The little man finishes his glass and slaps down a gleaming gold coin on the table. The waiter responds immediately and delivers a full bottle of wine and another glass to the table.

The small man gets another squeeze and more kisses as he fills the two glasses.

Chapter 62

In Giacomo's room the fourth bottle is being drained. Dante is still on the floor and Giacomo is propped up on his pile of pillows.

Both men are quite drunk and an air of sadness has descended on them. Dante is morose and wrestling with lurid images in his mind.

"I cannot believe that she would do this Giacomo."

He holds up his hand as Giacomo begins to speak.

"I know she loves me. She said so, many times."

"My friend, at the end of the day it is entirely your problem. Can you live with her knowing she may have betrayed you? Are you so stupid, so in love that you can bear those images? Every time she looks at you, will you not see her looking at some other man? Any man that can give her what she needs, her drug?"

A small tear begins to trickle down Dante's face as he takes the last drains from his glass.

"I love her. What can I do, Giacomo?"

At that moment Giacomo's small very drunk friend bursts through the door and stops short as he immediately senses the situation.

Giacomo asks him, "Did you deliver the food to the woman?"

The man shakes his head.

"Tried to, near knocked my knuckles raw before they heard me. They were playing violins, badly. When they stopped they must have heard me. Then the door was opened by a big fella, clutching his shirt."

He looks at Dante.

"Looked a bit like him, but with long yellow hair. I thought he was going to hit me at first but he just took the food and gave me a gold coin."

He holds out his hand to show the remains of his new found wealth, a collection of very small coins.

"I liked him."

Giacomo slowly turns to a distraught Dante.

"There my friend is your answer."

Chapter 63

Almost out of breath and sweating heavily from running, Dante eventually reaches the top landing outside his front door. Quietly he tries the key in the lock. The key turns but the door is bolted from the inside. He puts his ear to the door but can hear nothing. He tries the lock again. The door is still bolted. Dante smacks his open palm against the door several times. Now he can hear a scuffling and then a man's muffled voice.

"Who is it?"

He takes a deep breath to calm his breathing and then answers.

"Dante."

The bolt on the inside is quickly slid back and the door swings open to reveal Antonio who smiles as he moves to one side to allow Dante to enter.

"You?"

Antonio steps back into the room and walks over to the table where he pours some wine into a glass.

"Yes, Dante. Me, your old friend and recent benefactor."

Dante moves into the room and looks around.

"Where is she?"

Before answering, Antonio takes a drink of wine.

"She, the lovely Luisa?"

"Of course. Where is she? When I left she was sleeping."

Antonio laughs softly, almost to himself.

"She has gone."

A mystified Dante moves across to the small chest of drawers beside the bed. All of the drawers are pulled out and empty. He spins round to Antonio.

"What do you mean, gone?"

Picking up his wine glass, Antonio sweeps his arm around the room.

"Left, departed, vamoosed, vacated."
He drinks.
"How many ways can I describe her non presence?"
Anger begins to overwhelm Dante along with a feeling of danger.
"She was ill, incapable of going anywhere."
Moving to the small window, Antonio gazes outside as he speaks.
"She said to thank you."
"What?"
Again he is smiling as he turns to face Dante.
"For the fish. It was excellent. We did wait for you but you seemed reluctant to return from your little shopping trip. So we ate, played a little music, packed her bags and off she went."
"Impossible. You are lying. She would never do that."
Antonio points to the small table where the remnants of a meal are still there.
"No lies. See, there are the bones. Delicious."
A still angry Dante retorts.
"Not that. About her leaving."
Once again Antonio sweeps his hand to indicate the room.
"Am I? Can you see her?"
"Where has she gone?"
"A long way away, I'm afraid."
Dante moves closer to him.
"How do you know that? When will she back?"
Antonio pours out two glasses of wine before he answers. He hands one to Dante who ignores the offer.
"Questions, Dante. Always questions."
"Answer me."
Antonio takes a drink as he considers his answer.
"Last one first. She will not be back."
He takes another drink and looks intently at Dante.
"Ever."
This stuns Dante and he leans against the table.
Antonio continues.

"First question. How do I know?" He smiles.

"Her father told me."

Dante shakes his head in disbelief.

"Her father? He abandoned her, put her into that terrible place you sent me to. Why would he want her back now?"

Antonio sits on the low window ledge and looks out.

"It would seem he had a business arrangement, with the father of a drooling imbecile boy. The seal was Luisa's hand in marriage, which he shall have very soon."

He turns back to look at Dante.

"She will enjoy living in the Orient, and will be well on her way. Her vessel sailed on the turn of the tide, an hour or so ago."

Dante can barely think.

"The Orient? No. Where?"

He moves around the table to face Antonio.

"I must find her. How did her father know she was here, in this place?"

"Oh, that's a simple one Dante. I told him. Even brought him here. All at some cost of course. It seems he went to the Monastery and they informed him I was the most likely person to know of her whereabouts."

Slamming his hand on the table in anger Dante says, "You *sold* her?"

Antonio shakes his head.

"Hardly. She went back into the loving arms of her father. What is to sell? I merely made a charge for information."

"She loved me; she would never have left willingly."

A smiling Antonio nods his head in agreement.

"Quite right. She did put up a bit of resistance. Took three men to get her down the stairs. She did curse you a little tho'.

He laughs.

"Kept screaming for you, wanted to know where you were. Her loving father sent a warning to you. If you pursue her, he will kill her and then you."

He leans forward to Dante.

"Where were you?"

A still stunned Dante almost mumbles his answer.

"Visiting a friend, a sick friend."

"Ah, how noble. What ails him?"

"It is of no importance right now but he has a few bruises, some hurt pride and is missing a part of his anatomy."

"Really, how painful. Which part?"

Before answering, Dante pours some wine into a glass and then takes a sip as he considers his reply.

"That part you are already familiar with."

Antonio is completely unfazed by this and calmly finishes his wine. Draining the glass in one swallow, he bangs it down on the table and gives another little laugh.

"Would that be the codpiece from that odious dwarf Giacomo Grande?"

He continues laughing as he walks to the curtained window where he becomes almost a silhouette against the strong light as he looks out.

Dante speaks softly.

"You misbegotten creature. You sold Luisa and you stole his diamonds."

Without turning and still looking out, Antonio answers.

"What does a dwarf need diamonds for? He probably stole them himself. Anyway, I can make better use of them."

"Of course, to help finance your supply of Opium. Obviously your supply of ex nuns was not enough."

Antonio burst out laughing and turns from the window.

"How very melodramatic. Do grow up, Dante."

"She told you, didn't she? About the stones?"

Antonio nods.

"Of course."

He turns to look at Dante.

"It is amazing what some people will trade when you have something they desperately need."

Fighting an overwhelming urge to strike Antonio, Dante moves to the other side of the table.

"Like those poor lost souls in the mountains."

A laugh bursts out from Antonio.

"Do not be stupid, Dante. They did not need my merchandise. All they wanted was freedom. They were desperate to leave the place. Some had been there since childhood. I merely opened the door for them."

"With the help of that demented woman, the Mother Superior?"

A frown swiftly crosses Antonio's face.

"Of course, she chose the likely ones. She taught them the rudiments of playing the violin and then presented the best ones for selection. Anyway, I thought it would be a diversion for you, get you away from cloying domesticity and out of here for a while."

He looks around the small room.

"You caused a few problems returning when you did."

"So it was always planned to leave Luisa alone, to enable her father to remove her?"

"Yes, the vessel had to leave today. The tide, winds and profitable commerce wait for no man."

"So if I had not visited Giacomo, I would have been here."

"Very likely, and probably dead. Luisa's father is quite a rough person. Always gets what he wants."

"He might have met his match."

"He may have done but he had six men with him. I doubt even your farmer honed muscles would have won the day."

Out of the corner of his eye, Dante notices a leather bag at the foot of the very rumpled bed and walks over to it to look inside. The contents are a dozen or so small green bottles. Without another word, he swings the bag in a wide arc and smashes it onto the wooden floor where the sound of the smashing glass causes Antonio to swiftly move away from the window and leap across the room.

Liquid is seeping from the bag where Dante has thrown it and Antonio kneels to grab it up from the floor.

"You fool," he yells as he rips open the top.

Shards of green glass pour out along with liquid as he reaches in to try to salvage any unbroken bottles. There are none. All are now smashed. Throwing the sodden bag to one side, Antonio suddenly lets out a low growl as he launches himself against Dante.

As they wildly careen around the room, the cheap furniture is smashed and savage blows are landed by each man. Soon blood begins to mingle with the opium on the floor.

Finally Dante manages to catch Antonio with a blow to the face that makes him fall to the ground where his head connects sharply with the blood and opium spattered wood. He rolls over and lies still.

An exhausted Dante staggers to the bed to sit and wipe some blood from his face with a bed sheet. It is then that he notices a violin sticking out from under the bed. It is Luisa's. He bends to pull it out but it is still in its open case and it catches on the wooden base of the bed.

On the floor Antonio begins to revive and seeing what is happening on the bed picks up the shattered remnants of a wooden stool and sneaks up on Dante. He raises the stool above his head in order to strike him.

Suddenly the door bursts open and the small figure of Giacomo Grande dashes into the room. Performing a graceful forward roll in order to pick up speed the small man launches himself into the air to catch Antonio square in the chest with both of his feet.

Antonio is sent reeling across the room, still holding the heavy wooden stool above his head. His legs hit the low window parapet and he struggles to maintain his balance, but the weight of the stool works against him and he begins to fall out of the small window.

Just in time Antonio manages to grab the wooden frame at the side of the window and slowly pulls himself back inside the room. Then Giacomo strikes again. He runs across the room and sweeps Antonio's feet from under him. With a gasp of fear the violinist begins to drop.

Just as he is about to plummet, Giacomo reaches up as if to save him but he is really grabbing the small bag that is tied to Antonio's belt. For a moment or two Antonio's fall is delayed, but just by the time Giacomo needs to slice through the leather ties with his sharp stiletto blade.

This is all watched by Dante on the bed. A moment later comes the dreadful sound from outside of a body hitting something hard. There is a moment of silence as the horror of it sinks in. Dante painfully raises himself from the bed and moves across to the window.

There on a small terrace below them lies the now completely unconscious figure of Antonio, one of his arms twisted at a bad angle beneath him.

Giacomo holds up Antonio's leather purse and starts to dance a little jig.

"All of them. They are all here. He hasn't had time to sell them."

Dante ignores Giacomo's comments.

"He is still alive. It looks like he may have broken his arm."

Giacomo laughs.

"A one armed fiddler. Not much call for one of those."

He moves to a small chest and pulls open the drawers.

"Let's go, Dante. He wants to kill you. There's no baby and she never loved you."

He begins stuffing some of Dante's clothes into a cotton bag.

"There would be no harmony in this place."

He hands the half-filled bag to Dante.

"Leave now."

Dante is torn. He can hear voices outside on the balcony below and he moves to look out of the window again. A woman is cradling Antonio's head in her lap and she is accompanied by the other startled occupants of the building who all stand and stare at their unexpected guest.

Antonio's arm is still at a very odd angle and he is obviously in some pain.

"We must leave here now, Dante. Now."

Giacomo tugs at Dante's sleeve. The young violinist is mesmerized by the scene below and stubbornly refuses to move.

"He tried to kill you, Dante. He has helped to take away your woman. Leave him. Come now."

The sense of urgency in Giacomo's voice seems to snap the spell and Dante turns from the window.

Giacomo keeps pulling at his sleeve and they leave the building to hurriedly make their way down the rickety stairs to the alleyway.

Chapter 64

Early the following morning Dante slips quietly out of the rear door at the Palazzo Rialto where he spent a very uncomfortable night sleeping on a sofa in Giacomo's room. He makes his way swiftly through the maze of narrow calle and alleyways until he reaches a corner opposite Luisa's building and stands in a doorway where he can see but not be seen .

He waits patiently as the passages becomes active with early morning pedestrians, all too busy to give him any attention as he focuses on watching the building opposite. The curtains on the window where Antonio fell from are pulled across but Dante can see a movement in the room through the thin gauze.

Suddenly the curtains are pulled roughly apart and an unkempt looking Antonio appears. His arm is in a sling and he is gesticulating angrily to someone in the room. As Dante pulls further back into the doorway someone appears behind Antonio and appears to speak to him. The person is roughly pushed to one side as Antonio goes back into the room.

He watches for a few more moments and then leaves to make his way down the narrow deserted alley to the Port Registrar offices on the quayside at the eastern side of the city.

Chapter 65

The information from the Registry clerk did not make Dante any happier. There had been four foreign owned vessels that had set sail on the previous day's afternoon tide: one destined for India; one for the Americas by way of Cuba and two that had not filed destinations. None of them had registered any passengers.

Like a lost soul Dante moves through the calle of Venice. He is reluctant to go back to Giacomo's room so he spends the day in various coffee houses and taverns, avoiding the places he frequented in his early days in the city. Towards dusk he finds himself outside the Chapel of Santa Maria.

The chapel is almost deserted at this hour with only a few worshippers sitting in the long wooden pews. He enters and makes his way to where the candles are and lights one. He then takes a seat where he is almost completely on his own. A fat old monk enters the Chapel from a door at the side of the altar and walks towards the entrance. He stops when he reaches the pew where Dante is sitting and looks at him. Then he leans over to speak.

"Are you the Gabriele boy?"

Dante is lost in his own thoughts and is startled when he hears the priest speak to him.

"Yes, that is my family name."

"The boy who gave me a letter to post to his uncle, Father Emanuele, in Ebosta?"

A surprised Dante answers.

"Yes."

The fat monk squeezes into the pew and sits next to him.

"I have been looking for you. Where have you been?"

"Here. Here in Venice."

The monk peers at him and then in a slightly admonishing voice he continues.

"But not attending church."

Dante shakes his head and avoids the man's gaze.

"I have been too busy, Father, with many other things. But I promise I will be here more often."

The monk smiles to himself.

"What you do with your immortal soul is entirely up to you. No need to promise me anything."

He points upwards with a finger.

"That's the one to make promises to."

Dante nods and the monk starts talking again.

"You may have a good contact there."

He turns to look at the Monk who is still speaking.

"Some time ago I received a letter signed by your mother to inform you that your uncle, Father Emanuele, had passed away, working in the fields apparently."

He shakes his head.

"Priests are not farmhands. I could not find you so I opened the letter myself."

The news strikes Dante like a sword and he drops onto his knees, trying to say a prayer between stifling his sobs. The monk places his hand on his shoulder, and still sitting, he joins the young man in his prayer.

Chapter 66

The candles Dante lit are now almost burned down and the fat old monk has gone. Dante barely notices as he rises from his prayer position and sits back on the wooden seat of the pew. Tears are still slowly tickling down his face as he stares at the small altar of the chapel.

After a few moments, he opens his violin case, carefully wipes the polished wood of the instrument and then places it under his chin.

The strains of the Largo from Vivaldi's L' Inverno begin to fill the church. The few remaining worshippers turn in their seats to look at the young musician who is paying this tribute to his uncle, the very man who had taught him how to play the violin and had even given him the instrument. This was Emanuele's favourite piece of music and it restarts the tears that now flood down Dante's face.

When the music comes to an end, one old woman rises from her pew near the front of the church and walks up the aisle. When she reaches Dante she kisses the tips of her fingers and gently places them briefly on his shoulder. With a broad smile on her ancient wrinkled face she walks out of the church into the fading evening light.

Dante watches her go, puts the violin in its case and follows her out of the Chapel into the darkened calle of Venice.

Chapter 67

Four months later... Venice

The bitterly cold winter wind from Russia is sweeping over the nearby Dolomites and whistling down the narrow calle. Not many gondolas are out on the choppy waters and the local inhabitants who are abroad are well wrapped against the numbing chill.

Just a few days to go before the Christmas season begins. Most of the coffee houses and taverns are excelling themselves with enticing offers displayed on boards outside their well-lit doors. Those establishments that have windows looking out onto the alley have crammed their small paned frames with candles. Their warm inviting glow spills out onto the wet and icy passage ways.

It is early evening and already revelers are braving the weather to join in the celebrations. Little groups of four or five dash along, the men holding onto their flamboyant hats and the ladies trying to keep their voluminous dresses tucked under their long fur trimmed cloaks.

The mood of celebration in that ancient trading city is in the air and the excitement seems to be catching. Except in one small corner of an usually busy calle that has a number of popular taverns dotted along it. Whilst the taverns are packed, outside sits a lone violinist whose fingers are wrapped in some old cotton gloves, worn through at the fingers and whose thin cloak which should be around his shoulders is spread out on the ground to catch any carelessly thrown coins.

The fiddler is not playing very well, mainly because of the cold, and there are no coins on his cloak. He stops momentarily as a large group of boisterous revelers burst round the corner and crowd around the entrance of the tavern opposite him.

The Countess Margarethe of Waldstadten and her entourage already seem to be very drunk and in high spirits, particularly the one she is hanging on to as they push through into the tavern. Antonio is almost unrecognizable. His long blonde hair is swept up into a bouffant style and his cheeks are red with rouge. He also seems to be incapable of standing upright and the ageing countess has to place her arm around his waist as they disappear into the warm interior.

As Dante watches, a small coin lands on his cloak. He quickly bends to pick it up, aware that even beggars can be the target of other beggars in these hard times. As he straightens up and prepares to begin playing again he is aware of a figure standing just behind him. He turns and comes face to face with Giacomo Grande.

The dwarf smiles at him as he bends down and begins to gather up Dante's cloak.

"It is a long time my friend since we parted and you left to become a great musician or die in the attempt."

Dante stares at him in an almost trance like state as Giacomo continues.

"I think you may be reaching the end of your quest. You are near death, Dante."

"No."

Dante almost croaks the words.

"I must keep playing. I have to save some money to go and find Luisa."

Giacomo shakes his head.

"You are not making enough to even feed yourself. I only found out where you were by friends telling me you were sleeping in the calle. You must give this up, Dante. It is futile."

"Nothing is futile."

His words are cut short as a fierce blast of ice cold wind whips around the small square. He turns his back into it as he continues.

"I will find her and bring her back."

Giacomo squats down beside him and puts some of his cloak over his shoulders before saying quietly, "She is dead, Dante."

What he says makes no impression on the half frozen musician so he repeats himself.

"She is dead."

Dante slowly turns to look at Giacomo, his eyes begin to mist over and he shakes his head.

'If I could have found you earlier I would have told you, but I heard the Countess knows about the stones so I have been hiding in Pordenone. I came back a few days ago."

"I cannot believe it, Giacomo. Dead? How? When?"

"Apparently some fishermen out in the gulf saw a woman fall or jump overboard from a vessel, soon after we had the fight with Antonio. They looked for her but found nothing. Then a body, or what was left of it, was washed up on the edge of the lagoon."

"It could have been anyone. Why do you think it was Luisa?"

"The body they found was still wrapped in a blue silk robe, like the one she always wore. It has to be her, Dante."

It takes a few moments for Dante to absorb the awful truth of Giacomo's statement and he slumps even further down onto the pavement.

"She loved me; she must have tried to escape, to come back to me."

He starts sobbing gently as Giacomo grabs him and begins to pull him back up.

"If you do not get up Dante then your wish to see her soon may be granted. But not if I have my way. One life lost in this tale is one too many. Get up. We are in great danger Dante and they will hang us both."

Dante offers no resistance as Giacomo places the thin cloak over his shoulders.

"Come with me, my friend. I know a much better safer place for you than this."

Dante begins to rise and slightly staggers as his numb muscles refuse to co-operate. Giacomo puts his arm around him and they make their way along the alley and out of the icy cold blast that is now sweeping the square.

From the tavern opposite a very drunken Antonio lurches through the doors and leans against a wall. Frantically reaching into his pocket, he pulls out a little green bottle and tips his head back to drain it. As he does so he spots a man being helped along the alleyway going from the square by what appears to be a dwarf. The sight seems to momentarily make him sober and he hurriedly stumbles back into the tavern.

Chapter 68

A week later

The room is large, with two broad beds and several couches. Outside the small framed windows the snow is falling heavily but the big log fire which blazes away in the inglenook fireplace has made the room very warm. Wrapped up in a woollen blanket and sitting facing the fire is Dante. He is seemingly mesmerized by the sparks from the logs which rise slowly and disappear up the broad chimney. He is startled slightly as Giacomo Grande suddenly appears from behind the high backed chair.

"Still snowing out there. We will have to wait another day or so before we continue to your family farm."

A weak nod from Dante.

"That is not a bad thing. I need to recover some more, Giacomo, otherwise my mother will faint. When I left home I was fit and healthy. Now look at me."

Giacomo pulls up a small stool and sits beside the chair.

"You will be fine. Some more of the good food here and some sleep and all will be well."

The two men stare into the flames then Dante asks.

"The journey here and these lodgings, Giacomo, how are we going to pay? That was a fine carriage that brought us here."

Giacomo gives a little laugh.

"A fine carriage indeed, worthy of a Cardinal, one who owes me many favours! And I sold another stone, so do not concern yourself about money, Dante. It is all taken care of."

Dante turns to look at him.

"Why?"

The response is slow as Giacomo considers his words, and still looking into the flames he finally answers.

"Because you are my friend."

"We hardly know each other and we have had some disagreements."

Again Giacomo waits before answering.

"A friendship, a true friendship, can be forged in a moment, Dante. I knew you would be an influence in my life from the first time I saw you play."

"And then you stole my violin. Some friend!"

Turning slowly away from the fire Giacomo turns to face him.

"I took it because I knew it would bring you after me, and it did. I wanted to have you in my life as a friend because you are the very first human being to treat me with respect, as an equal. My size means nothing to you. That is the first time in my life that I have experienced that. I wanted more of it."

"I never gave it any thought. You were just a thief, a small one admittedly, and you did save my life.

"Three times, my friend." They both smile at this then Giacomo continues.

"You are a simple person, Dante. An innocent in a wicked world. You see only the best in everyone. To me that is unique, and really rather wonderful. Almost Holy."

He laughs and begins to rise.

"Now I need to eat. The inn is empty so I shall go to the kitchens and see what is there and bring some back for you. We also need some more wood. I will kick the innkeeper's arse and send him in with some."

He walks briskly to the door and as it closes behind him Dante almost immediately begins to doze off.

Chapter 69

A lone horseman crests the high hill leading to the inn, which is not showing many lights, mainly because there are few travellers willing to brave the driving snow and chilling cold. The horse's hooves make almost no noise on the trail and not even when it enters the cobbled stone courtyard.

The heavily clothed rider makes his way directly to the big open sided barn and stable block. Quickly dismounting he ties the horse to a rail and then carefully takes a look around in the semi darkness.

He moves silently across the courtyard and steps into the deep doorway. He tries the door which is firmly locked. He then begins to creep around the perimeter of the building.

A row of small windows run along one of the walls and the rider takes care when he peers into what appears to be a kitchen. Large stoves with some boiling pans and a roaring fire tell him that someone is using it. He creeps below the window sill and moves further round the large property.

A moment later Giacomo walks into the kitchen with a wire basket of eggs which he places on the worktop, then busies himself looking for utensils in a drawer.

Chapter 70

Dante is dozing slightly when the door to the room opens slowly. He settles down further into the warmth and comfort of his chair.

Giacomo's little stool is pulled up closer and Dante blinks his eyes open to see the face of Antonio just a few inches away from his. Between the two of them is a very sharp pointed dagger blade. Antonio forces a smile.

"Hello, fiddler. Remember me?"

Even in his weakened state Dante tries to sit up but the blade under his chin stops him.

"What do you want?"

"Not a lot, fiddler. Just what is really mine. Some small stones. Do you remember them as well?"

"They are not yours."

Still smiling Antonio puts more pressure on the blade.

"Exactly. They really belong to the crone but I need them to get away from her and my need is greater than the dwarf's. So, where is he?"

"Not here."

Antonio begins to stand up.

"Do not take me for an idiot, Dante. He brought you here in the Cardinal's fine coach. Another thing he could be hanged for. The Cardinal is already screaming that his coach was stolen. When I reach Rome I will be telling the authorities where to find the pair of you, or your bodies."

"The coach was a loan."

Antonio bursts out laughing.

"What a fool you are, Dante."

He suddenly turns serious.

"Now, where is he? I need to get the stones and now. Since you broke my arm I have never played again. I had to become that woman's toy, her sex toy. All my money has been spent tracking you two to this place."

He places the dagger across Dante's throat.

"But I have a bigger score to settle with you my friend and I want to see you hang on the gibbet for that one."

"What are you talking about?"

The point of the blade digs deeper into Dante's neck as Antonio leans into him.

"Murder, farm boy. Cold blooded murder. And witnesses to swear your life away."

Dante is hoarse as he answers.

"Murder? What murder?"

Antonio pushes his face as close as he can get to Dante's.

"The murder of a Saint, a beautiful woman. You sent her to her death and the nuns will vouch for it. They saw you kill my mother."

Stunned, Dante takes his time in answering.

"The Mother Superior was your mother?"

Antonio's voice hardens.

"The mother I found after many years of searching. The mother you pushed over the wall to her death. You murdered her."

Dante tries to shake his head but the blade digs a little deeper.

"She fell. She tripped and fell. She was trying to say something about *me* not having *them*. I don't know what she meant. I tried to save her."

"I told her that Luisa was having my child, that you wanted to take them away from me."

"Why did you lie? The baby was not yours."

"My mother wanted to leave the nunnery. I told her she could after the child was born. Then we could all have a home together. She had to stay there. She had to keep the place open for a while longer."

"For more of your deals, selling young nuns into slavery for opium?"

"I just needed one more big delivery, then it would stop."

Dante manages a slight smile.

"You are totally insane, Antonio. The drugs have rotted your brain. You lost Luisa to me, told your beloved mother a lie, drove her to distraction and we have lost both of them."

"You lie. Your word against thirty devout nuns, Dante. Who would you believe? Who will the judges believe? You will hang for it and I will be there to see it. Now tell me, Dante, or I won't wait for the hangman. I will finish you right here."

At that moment the door is pushed open and a man backs into the room. He is carrying a pile of logs and as he turns round he sees Antonio and the knife at Dante's neck.

"You!"

Signor Angelo Nadalini is so shocked at what he sees that he drops the logs onto the floor. At the same time, Dante manages to push Antonio's hand away from his throat. He rolls across the floor and grabs one of the longer logs which he holds up in front of himself.

Antonio moves across the room to confront him, waving the long bladed knife in front of him. Angelo keeps to one side and flattens himself against the wall as the two armed men begin to move slowly round the room with Antonio making parrying and stabbing motions. Sweat is now running freely down Dante's face as the heavy log is rapidly draining his strength.

Dante backs his way round to the door but as he almost reaches it, he steps on one of the fallen logs which rolls out from under his foot and stumbles.

Antonio seizes the chance and leaps forward with a wild slash of the knife. The blade sinks deeply into the log Dante is carrying and he twists at it, forcing the knife from Antonio's grasp. The two men begin to grapple as they crash around the room. Antonio manages to get his hand on the knife handle again and wrenches it free just as Dante falls backwards over the stool. Both of them, still locked together begin to roll across the floor.

Antonio manages to force the point of the blade towards Dante's face as they roll and then he manages to sit astride him with one knee. Holding Dante's arm against the floor, he pushes against the weaker man with all of his strength.

Giacomo opens the door carrying a tray of food which he instantly throws to one side and jumps on Antonio's back. He begins to dig his fingers into the violinist's eyes and this forces Antonio to fall backwards, swinging the sharp blade in a wide arc.

Giacomo, in spite of being much smaller, is extremely strong and he manages to grab hold of the hand holding the knife as they struggle. Dante staggers to his feet as the two fighters begin to roll towards the fireplace.

Giacomo's back makes contact with the thick metal cradle that holds the burning wood and it begins to burn through his jacket. He yells as the hot metal touches his bare back, and he desperately begins to push back at Antonio who has another slash at him as he gets up on one knee.

He begins to make stabbing motions towards Giacomo who is now pinned beneath him and begins to snarl at the same time.

"Where are my stones, you thieving little bastard? Where are they?"

Giacomo, in a desperate move to get away from the hot metal now searing his back, suddenly reaches up and tries to pull Antonio to one side. At the same time an almost petrified Angelo grabs one of his fallen logs and steps forward to smack the thick and heavy piece of wood onto the back of Antonio's head.

Almost in slow motion Antonio begins to roll over and away from Giacomo who falls to the ground and squirms away from the fireplace.

Antonio slowly crumples to the floor and all three of them stare silently as a pool of dark red blood begins to form on the floor beneath his head.

Angelo backs away in shock and horror as Dante manages to fall back into his chair. Giacomo is now leaning against the wall next to the fireplace.

"Is he dead?" a quivering Angelo asks.

Gathering all of his strength, Dante drops to the floor on his knees and makes his way to Antonio where he feels for a heartbeat. On trying to turn the man's body over, the knife is uncovered. The blade is bloody and Dante pushes it to one side. One look at Antonio's face tells him that he is dead and he slowly lowers the body to the floor.

"Yes."

Wiping his sweating face with the bottom of his apron, Angelo whispers, "My god, I've killed him."

Giacomo coughs slightly as he speaks in a weak voice.

"Someone had to do it. He was lucky to last this long."

Dante looks at him.

"What are we going to do? We could all hang for this."

A silence descends as they all consider their predicament. Angelo is the first to speak.

"We have to get rid of him. Get rid of his body. No-one knows about this except us."

"There are two thieves, one killer and a dead man in this room. Who would take our word that he attacked us?" says Dante.

Giacomo speaks up from his position by the fire.

"Two killers and one thief, Dante."

Dante slowly turns to look at him, slightly mystified by what he has said. Then he notices the large dark patch of blood spreading from under Giacomo. With a new found energy he moves quickly across to his friend who just smiles at him.

"Angelo killed Antonio and Antonio killed me." He moves his hands which are clutching at his stomach and a gout of blood spurts out.

"He finally got me, Dante."

He tries to laugh but is stopped by a short coughing spasm.

"But he never got these."

With one hand he pulls a small leather pouch from inside his doublet and presses it into Dante's hand.

"Take these, my friend. Do whatever you need to do with them. This little man's life no longer needs them."

A shocked Dante takes the pouch and begins to speak, but Giacomo motions for him to stop.

"You are a true friend, Dante, and a good man. Put this behind you."

He reaches out to touch Dante's face but his hand falls back.

Suppressing a sob, Dante puts his arms around him and pulls him close. Giacomo begins to cough as he is pulled up and his face is now leaning on Dante's shoulder.

"There is something you must know, Dante," he whispers. "Please forgive me, but I have to tell you a secret."

Dante relaxes his hold on the little man and looks into his face as Giacomo begins to speak again. But Dante stops him.

"It will wait, Giacomo. Right now we must get you better."

Giacomo shakes his head as a coughing spell overwhelms him and in the midst of it large gouts of blood pour from his mouth. He never finishes what he has to say and dies in Dante's arms.

Chapter 71

The large logs that were burning in the fireplace are now just embers and cast out just a little warmth to the two distraught men sitting in front of it.

The bodies of Giacomo and Antonio are still where they fell and are covered in sheets from the bed.

Angelo passes over the almost empty bottle of Brandy to Dante and then motions to the two dead men.

"We have to get rid of them, and all trace of them being here."

Dante nods.

"True. How do you suggest we do that?"

Angelo is quiet for a moment then answers.

"We have just dug a large pit for the pig and cattle slurry and it takes the stable sweepings. We use it for manure on the fields. It's behind the barn."

Shaking his head Dante replies.

"Do what you will with Antonio, but the little man comes home with me. He will have a proper funeral and resting place."

Angelo considers this for a moment then begins to rise, rather unsteadily, to his feet.

"Done. Are you able to give me a hand?"

Dante takes a long drink from the bottle before answering.

"Yes, best get it over with and when dawn comes I will depart for my home."

The two very drunk men move to where Antonio's body is and begin to wrap it in some more bedding.

Chapter 72

The thick snow makes it easy for Angelo and Dante to slide the sheet wrapped body of Antonio from the inn to the rear of the barn to where the slurry pit is.

Even in the half light of the night it is possible to see the small bubbles of gas breaking on the surface of the dark brown coloured lagoon. The pit measures some twenty yards square and is surrounded by high earth mound walls.

Dragging the body to the top of the mound, they begin to unwrap it from its cocoon of blankets.

Antonio lies face up and does not look as though he is dead. But rigor mortis is already setting in and as both men take a deep breath and begin to roll the violinist's corpse down the slight embankment, Antonio's stiff arms stop its slide. Angelo looks at Dante and then realises he has to finish the job. He carefully clambers down beside the body to give it one final push into the quagmire.

He scrambles back to the top to witness Antonio's face slowly disappearing into the slurry. Within seconds he has gone leaving only a slight disturbance on the thick oily surface.

Chapter 73

The Cardinal's coach, with Dante in the driver's seat, stops at the top of the hill overlooking the Gabriele farm and comes to a halt.

After leaving the Nadalini inn at the crack of dawn, Dante had pushed the horse hard to get to his home as quickly as possible. Now he is but a minute or so away.

Smoke is rising from the farmhouse chimney and there are fresh footprints in the thin layer of snow that lies in the stable yard. Dante gently urges the tired horse forward and the coach makes its way slowly down the slight incline.

Finally, pulling to a halt in the yard, Dante climbs stiffly down from the driver's seat and leans against the polished woodwork of the gilded coach. He can hear voices from inside the building and one of the thin curtains at the window is briefly pulled to one side.

Dante's mother is the first one to appear through the doorway and without saying a word she dashes across to her son and embraces him as tears begin to flow down her face.

Franco is next in the doorway where he just stands and watches before being pushed roughly aside by the rest of the family as they all mill around a grinning Dante.

Eventually Franco walks across to his eldest boy and puts his arms around him as he leads him back into the warmth of the kitchen.

* * *

Dante's timing had been perfect. He had arrived just at the end of the midday meal and he lost no time in devouring the leftovers. Refusing all of his mother's attempts to prepare him fresh food, he hungrily devoured the remnants of a robust soup and several small fresh baked loaves. Only when he had finished and sits back in his chair do the inevitable questions begin. But first he asks them about his uncle Emanuele.

Franco recalls that terrible day without going into much detail.

"He just fell down in the mud and died, son. It must have all been too much for him. He always said he was not a farmer."

Bruno takes up the tale.

"We made a coffin from the oak tree, the one he helped us saw up."

Dante is silent for a few moments and then he looks at Bruno.

"Is there any of that wood left? Enough for another coffin, a small one?"

Slightly mystified, Bruno looks at his father then back to Dante.

"Yes. But why do you need a coffin, and a small one."

"For a friend, a very good friend. I want him to have a proper grave in a proper coffin."

His mother holds her apron to her face and asks the inevitable question.

"Who is this friend? Where is he? Is he dead?"

Dante stands up and walks to the window where he looks out at the coach and horse which are still standing in the farmyard.

"His name is Giacomo. He is dead and he is in the back of that coach."

Turning to his father and brother, he says, "Bruno, go and sort out the timber. Father, can you help me with him?"

He indicates the Cardinal's coach.

"And we must destroy every piece of that."

Franco is slightly taken aback at the speed of events.

"Of course. But why destroy the coach? It is a beautiful piece of work, fit for a prince."

A smiling Dante moves towards the door.

"That's why it must be destroyed. It actually belongs to a prince, one of the Catholic church's princes. It would soon be noticed if the Gabriele family were to turn up at the market place in a gilded coach."

He stops as he opens the door.

"It was stolen and I would be hanged for stealing it. Bring an axe and a spade father. We have work to do."

He walks out into the yard and begins to unharness the horse which he hands over to Bruno.

"She will need some food and water. Put her in the byre for now with Tessy."

Admiring the large horse, Bruno asks, "Whose is it, Dante?"

A little smile crosses Dante's face.

"It belonged to someone who has no need for it now. I suppose it belongs to us."

Franco peers into the window of the carriage.

"Your friend, where is he?"

Opening the door Dante answers the question by pointing to a large bundle of white sheets which are wrapped around Giacomo. His face is not covered and apart from looking pale he appears to be sound asleep.

"I placed him on the floor for the journey."

"He seems to be very small."

Anna had appeared and peers into the coach from behind Franco.

Closing the door, Dante turns to her.

"He is small only in height mother. And now we must give him a giant's funeral."

The rest of that short dark day is spent working on the thick planks of oak, stripping out the polished parts of the carriage to line the small coffin and the red silk padded seating to provide a bed in its base. Anything that cannot be used is burnt on a bonfire at the rear of the byre.

Bruno, who is a talented carpenter, is left to carry out this task as Franco and Dante walk up to the small churchyard behind the church.

* * *

The very old community of Ebosta has seen many deaths during its existence and the graveyard on the hillside overlooking the village is crammed full of ancient as well as recent gravestones.

Family plots are clearly designated and one or two small family vaults dominate the more choice areas. At one end of this craggy, rock strewn place of the dead there is one simple stone crucifix that seems to stand out. It is in a corner of the cemetery at the very top and it appears to have been placed to keep watch on all of the other monuments.

The almost constant breeze from the distant hills softly blows the long grass between the graves as Dante and his father stop in front of the simple headstone which is inscribed with the words

Father Emanuele Gabriele
Parish Priest

There are no other words, no family connection and no dates. The two men stand in silence for a few moments in silent prayer and then Dante moves to one side and digs the long handled spade into the soft earth.

"This is the place, father; this is where my friend will sleep."

Chapter 74

The funeral of Giacomo Grande took place early the following morning. Dante had kept a vigil in the small village church all night, occasionally playing his violin, walking around the open coffin, praying, and generally thinking about his life and future.

The church had never been open much since Father Emanuele had died and a mass was only held there once a month by a priest from another parish who rode into the village mid-afternoon, gave a short sermon, a very quick service and left within the hour. Any christenings, funerals and weddings had to be carried out in other parishes. Franco had taken on the responsibility of looking after the church. He and Anna swept it out once a week and made sure the building was secure.

Giacomo's funeral is the only one that has not had the services of a priest but Dante has learnt a few words for the funeral and he recites them to himself as he keeps vigil.

When dawn breaks Franco and Bruno arrive to help carry the small coffin to its resting place. When they arrive at the open grave, Anna joins them. It is too early for the younger children and no-one else in the village is aware there is a funeral taking place.

The four members of the Gabriele family stand at the grave side and Dante reads what he can remember of the funeral service. A moment's silence and then just before Bruno and his father begin to screw down the coffin lid Dante leans in and places Giacomo's battered old codpiece beside the small man.

All four take hold of the ropes and lower the coffin into the ground. When they leave to slowly make their way back to the farm house for a warm breakfast, Dante stays behind to say a last little prayer. Then he takes the long handled shovel and slowly fills in the grave.

When his task is complete he stands at the foot of the graves of the two men he loved and after a short prayer he walks back to join his family.

He has something very important to tell them.

* * *

Breakfast is a slightly sombre affair but everyone brightens up when the two smallest family members finally join them.

Just as Bruno and Franco prepare to leave for work in the fields, Dante asks them to give him a moment of their time. He has made a decision and wants them to hear it first.

He begins by asking them to destroy whatever was left of the Cardinal's carriage, to burn what can be burnt and utilize what can be useful. He also asks them to provide a simple headstone for Giacomo. He will pay. And then he tells them he will be leaving again, that day, and will be away for a considerable period of time. That he has something important that he must do but then he makes a solemn promise that one day when he has completed his mission he will return, never to leave them again.

Chapter 75

Three years later

It is a Saint's day in the village of Ebosta and the single bell in the tower of the church is being rung vigorously. Already on this Sunday morning the small square in front of the church is filling with villagers and people from the outlying district. Two of the small taverns are serving beverages and strong drinks to the more thirsty parishioners and there seem to be a lot of them.

As the bell suddenly stops ringing, all eyes turn to the front doors of the church as they slowly swing open for the first time in months.

The newly ordained Father Dante Gabriele blinks in the strong sunlight as he begins to usher his flock of worshippers into the church for his first ever mass as the new resident priest of the Parish of Ebosta

The mass is carried out and at the end Dante is asked by his new parishioners if he will carry out the tradition of his uncle Emanuele, that is to play some violin pieces. For some of them, it is the only time they actually hear any music at all, except for untrained musicians at weddings and birthday celebrations.

Dante obliges and plays for at least another hour.

Very happy parishioners pour out into the sunlit square and make their way home.

Anna presses Dante to join the family for a midday meal to celebrate the day and he happily agrees. But first he wants to visit the churchyard and say hello to two old friends.

The walk from the church to the top of the cemetery is a short one, but Dante takes his time, stopping at one or two burial plots, trying to put faces to names, before strolling on.

At last he arrives at the top of the small rise and stands in front of the two graves. Giacomo's now has a plain headstone with the carved words

Giacomo Grande
Giant
Friend

The graves are beautifully tended by his mother Anna, and fresh flowers are placed on both mounds. Dante says a little prayer and begins to turn away when the sun glints off something bright and metallic at the base of Giacomo's headstone.

Brushing aside the short grass, Dante begins to unfurl a silver chain at the bottom of which hangs a crucifix. His heart skips a beat as he realises this is the same crucifix that he had passed on to Luisa, the one the Mother Superior had been wearing as she fell over the monastery wall, the one that became entangled on the bow of his violin.

Sweat breaks out on his brow as he holds the religious emblem tight in his hand and slowly looks around.

Some small shrubs at the top of the graveyard bend slightly in the soft breeze and slightly obscure Dante's vision, but there at the top of the hill overlooking the village, some two hundred yards away, stands the figure of a tall woman. Her long brown hair and her silken skirts are blowing slightly in the gentle wind. At her feet is a handgrip and strapped to the top is a violin case. Holding her hand is a small child.

Dante can barely breath. He feels as if he has been struck by a bolt of lightning and he reels slightly. 'No, *it cannot be.*'

Holding the crucifix even more tightly he presses it to his forehead and slowly, almost fearfully, he looks back up the hill.

Part of his soul, his brain, wishes for a miracle; that the vision he had seen was from his memory, from somewhere deep in his psyche; he hoped at the very least for it to be a mirage.

He stares through the near shrubs. The woman and the child are still there. They are real.

Dante's heart is pumping so hard that it causes a roaring in his ears. He turns to the grave and whispers, "Giacomo Grande, giant friend and eternal liar!"

He smiles.

"An entertainer to the last. You must be enjoying this!"

He steps over the low stone wall that surrounds the cemetery and with quickening speed moves as fast as he can up the hill.

The end